"Lest There Be Any Misunderstanding, I'm Agreeing To This Arrangement Because I Want You In My Bed.

"Do you still want to come?" Garth added.

"Oh, I'm coming," Candy reassured him. "But I think you should know that I'm cured of the love or infatuation or whatever it was I felt for you three years ago. I won't set my heart on a platter and watch you refuse it again. You're welcome to do your best to seduce me. But I'd never sleep with a man I didn't love. If you're smart, you won't waste your time trying."

"It's my time," Garth said, infuriated. He thought he didn't want her love. Why would she think he cared whether she offered it to him? Candy's opposition only made the chase that much more interesting. She would give in sooner or later. He had never met a woman yet who hadn't.

Dear Reader,

Let's talk about summer—those wonderful months of June, July and August, when the weather warms up and Silhouette Desire stays hot.

June: Here is where you'll find another dynamite romance about the McLachlan brothers—this time Ross—by BJ James (look for more brothers later in the year!), a *Man of the Month* by Barbara Boswell, and another installment in the *Hawk's Way* series by Joan Johnston.

July: Don't look now but it's the *Red, White and Blue* heroes! These men are red-blooded, white-knight, blue-collar guys, and I know you'll love all of them! Look for the hero portrait on each and every one of these books.

August: It's a *Man of the Month* from Diana Palmer, a story from Dixie Browning and another delightful tale from Lass Small...and that's just a *tiny* amount of what's going on in August.

Yes, I think summer's going to be pretty terrific, and in the meantime I want to ask you all some questions. What do you think of the Desire line? Is there anything you'd particularly like to see that we don't provide? No answer is too outrageous; I *want* to hear your opinions.

So write and let me know. And yes, I really do exist! I'm not just some made-up name that goes on the bottom of these letters.

Until next month, happy reading,

Lucia Macro
Senior Editor

JOAN JOHNSTON

THE WRANGLER AND THE RICH GIRL

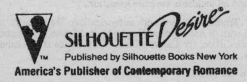

SILHOUETTE *Desire*®

Published by Silhouette Books New York

America's Publisher of Contemporary Romance

SILHOUETTE BOOKS
300 East 42nd St., New York, N.Y. 10017

THE WRANGLER AND THE RICH GIRL

Copyright © 1993 by Joan Mertens Johnston

ISBN: 0-373-05791-1

First Silhouette Books printing June 1993

Printed in the U.S.A.

JOAN JOHNSTON

started reading romances to escape the stress of being an attorney with a major national law firm. She soon discovered that writing romances was a lot more fun than writing legal bond indentures. Since then, she has published a number of historical and contemporary category romances. In addition to being an author, Joan is the mother of two children. In her spare time, she enjoys sailing, horseback riding and camping.

Prologue

"So how did Mom and Dad meet, Charlie?"

"That's a long story, Zach, and it's time for you three kids to get to bed." Charlie One Horse, the ancient part-Comanche housekeeper at Hawk's Way, ruffled the hair of the seven-year-old boy sitting on the rawhide stool at the foot of his chair. Zach Whitelaw was the spitting image of his father, Garth. He had black hair that hung over his forehead and dark brown eyes that could be equally serious and mischievous.

"I wanta hear, too," Falcon said. Garth's six-year-old son was stretched out on his belly in front of the fireplace, his head resting on his palms. He had his father's black hair, but his eyes were the same blue as his mother's. Falcon possessed bronzed skin, high cheekbones and a sharp blade of nose passed down from his Comanche great-great-grandmother.

"Me, too!" four-year-old Callen chorused. Garth's youngest child, the only girl, had her mother's delicate features, but her father's black hair and dark eyes. She wriggled around in Charlie's lap so she could see the old man's face. She put a hand on the Indian's weathered cheek and said, "Please, Charlie?"

Charlie glanced from the three children to their parents, who were sitting on the sofa across from him. Garth had his arm around Candy, and her blond head lay nestled against his shoulder. His big hand clasped hers. They were the image of a loving, caring couple. It hadn't always been that way.

"So you wanta hear how your mom and dad met, do you?"

"You bet!"

"Sure do!"

"Uh-huh!"

"And after I finish you'll all go to bed without arguin'?"

Three heads nodded vigorously.

"Well, now, let me see," Charlie began as he tugged on the rawhide that held one of his gray braids. He chose his words well, knowing there was no way he could tell those three innocent faces the truth. "Long about eight years ago, your father was a hoss wrangler, just like he is now. And your mother, why, she was a rich girl. One of them gen-u-ine Texas deb-u-tantes. Now, one day..."

Garth's hand tightened on Candy's as the old man began to speak. Their eyes met and held. As Charlie told a story of how they had met and fallen in love, the two of them remembered how it had really happened.

One

———

Garth Whitelaw had only one use for women, so he didn't have much to do with the decent sort, like the lady heading straight for him now. He avoided meeting the widely spaced, speculative gray eyes that sought him out along the show ring at the spring quarter horse sale in Amarillo. But he felt a definite tightening across his loins as he perused her long, jean-clad legs and sylphlike figure.

He couldn't help admiring the grace of her walk or the way her long blond hair shifted across her shoulders as she moved. His appreciation was balanced by the knowledge that where this particular woman was concerned, the growing bulge behind his fly had damn well better stay zipped in his jeans.

Candice Baylor was a genuine Texas debutante, the daughter of one of the richest men in the state. Garth had first met her three years ago, when she was seventeen. She and her father, Evan, had come to his northwest Texas ranch, Hawk's Way, to look over some championship cutting horses Garth had for sale.

Initially Garth had been amused when Candy tagged along behind him everywhere he went. He had a younger sister who had taught him patience, so he answered all Candy's eager questions with brotherly indulgence. Because she was clever and interested in everything he did, it was easy to be tolerant.

It soon became clear to Garth that his horses weren't the only thing that interested Candy Baylor. Unless he was very much mistaken, the girl had caught a bad case of puppy love. She began flirting with him, sending coy, come-hither looks from beneath lowered lashes.

Garth was annoyed by her antics because even though he knew what she was doing—and despite the fact that she was entirely too young for him—he had felt the first stirrings of arousal. He had scowled mightily at her, but even that hadn't discouraged her.

Garth frowned as he remembered how, the night before she was scheduled to leave the ranch, Candy had confronted him in the downstairs room that served as both office and parlor. She had been dressed for bed and wore a thigh-length belted aqua silk robe over matching long silk pajama bottoms. She might only have been seventeen, but Garth had seen a woman's shape beneath the sensually draped fabric.

Candy claimed she couldn't sleep and just needed someone to talk to. Garth had given her several crude, broad hints, but she hadn't left him alone. So he had settled back in his chair with a whiskey in hand to watch the show, certain he could handle anything this spoiled little rich girl could dish out.

Candy had wandered around the room touching his things—vicariously touching him. She sought out the collection of trophies he had won in cutting horse futurities and fingered the delicate designs. She picked up a photo of Garth with his two younger brothers, Faron and Jesse, and his sister, Tate, from the mantel and tenderly traced his image. Then she ran her hand the length of the pine mantel, which drew her slowly, inexorably toward where he sat in one of the two leather chairs that faced the stone fireplace.

Frustrated by the arousal he couldn't control, Garth fought fire with fire. As she stood before him, he let his gaze insolently run the length of her, stopping to admire the firm, high breasts and flat belly before following the length of her pajama-clad legs to her bare toes. When he looked back up at her face, she was blushing a fiery red.

But she didn't run. He felt a grudging respect for her because he knew the same look had warned off older, more savvy women. Candy had merely turned and strolled, hips sashaying, to the chair across from him. Instead of sitting down normally, she had curled herself into the leather chair with her feet underneath her. She had rested her elbows on the arm of the chair and cupped her chin in her hands.

"Why haven't you ever gotten married?" she asked.

Garth had fielded that question from a lot of women during his thirty-odd years. He gave her his usual cynical response. "Why buy the cow when the milk's free?"

She wrinkled her nose in disgust. "That's an awful thing to say! A man gets other things from marriage besides sex."

"There's nothing else I want or need from a woman."

"What about children?"

Garth's lips flattened. "If I could be sure they were mine, maybe I'd want some."

"What do you mean, if you could be sure they were yours? Whose else would they be?"

"Some other man's," Garth responded curtly.

"No wife of yours would—"

"You're right. No wife of mine would. I'd kill her first," Garth said in a harsh voice. "But don't fool yourself. Lots of wives cheat on their husbands." His own mother had cheated on his father. His younger brother—half brother—Faron had been the result.

"What about companionship?" Candy demanded. "A wife can be a friend, someone to share your hopes and dreams and troubles with."

"I've got lots of friends." He smirked and added, "Of course, none of them are women. I figure there are better things to do when you're with a woman than talk."

She blushed again, an enchanting pink flush that raised the ridge in his jeans. He was ready to concede the battle to her and leave the room, but she asked one more question.

"What about love?" she said in a quiet voice.

"What about it?"

"Haven't you ever been in love with a woman and wanted her to love you back?"

His lips curled in a sardonic smile. "I'm not the kind of man women fall in love with."

She swallowed hard and said, "I love you."

Her gray eyes were huge in her face. He had never seen such a look in a woman's eyes. This was different from the admiration of his physical body, his broad shoulders and narrow waist, his straight nose and mouth, his black hair and deep brown eyes, which he had often seen from the women who wanted him—for sex or his money or to show off on their arms. This was something more.

Garth felt a pain in his chest, like there was a great weight on it, making it hard to breathe. For one brief instant he wanted nothing more than to gather her up in his arms and hold her tight, to reach out and accept the love she offered.

But it was an instant only, and the fact he had even considered holding to his bosom what he knew was just one more female viper made him all the more harsh when he finally responded to her words of love.

"What you're feeling isn't love, little girl. It's good old-fashioned lust. Since you've been asking for it ever since you walked into this room, I figure it's about time you got it." He noticed his hand was shaking when he set down his whiskey glass, so he quickly balled it into a fist.

When he rose to his full height she looked up at him, frozen like a rabbit in a gunsight. Her face had bleached white and her hands had dropped into her lap. He reached out to grasp her wrists and slowly drew her to her feet.

Garth waited for Candy to stop him or show the least sign of fear or resistance. What he wanted her to do was run from him, back to her rich daddy, back to the safe haven of her room upstairs.

He was less surprised this time when she did not.

Candy laid her hands on his bare forearms. Then she turned her face up to his. Her innocent gray eyes were filled with love—and trust.

Garth had never felt so confused. His flesh burned where she touched him. Desire sent blood rushing through his body, engorging a shaft that was already rock hard. He wanted her like he had never wanted another woman. But he was equally determined that he wasn't going to take her. She was just a rich kid with a bad case of puppy love— which he was about to cure.

His mouth was hard, almost brutal, when it captured hers, and his tongue raped and ravaged the inside of her mouth.

Sweet. Dear God, she's so sweet!

Garth was disturbed and disgusted when he felt himself responding to the young girl in his arms. He was a bastard, but not enough of one to take advantage of a teenage virgin. He pressed his mouth harder against hers—hard enough to scare the bejesus out of her—until he tasted blood.

He felt her begin to struggle in his arms and reached out for her breast, the most crude, most possessive male gesture he could make. He cupped the warmth of her through the slippery silk, and in spite of the strong urge he felt to caress her, forced himself to tighten his hold beyond what a girl of her little experience would find comfortable. This wasn't making love. This was sex. Down and dirty. The kind he might have with a woman who wanted it a little rough.

"No, Garth!"

When Candy jerked away, he let her go. She nearly fell when he released her. She stood panting, her parted lips still moist and swollen from his kisses. Her eyes...her gray eyes were wounded, full of pain and disillusionment. She wiped her mouth with the back of her hand, leaving a streak of blood across her cheek. He felt acid in the pit of his stomach.

"Why?" she asked in a ragged voice. "I love—"

He cut her off with an obscene oath. "Don't use that word to me! Foolish little girl! You're just a rich kid playing grown-up. Come back and see me when you're woman enough to handle what I have to offer."

He kept his eyes hard, his lips curled into a sneer. Even then she hadn't run. He had watched the tears brim in her eyes, watched her try to blink them back before one finally spilled down her cheek. It was plain she wanted to say something to him, but she couldn't talk because she had her teeth gritted to control her trembling chin.

For several tense moments he stood there feeling an urgent need to comfort her. He forced himself to remain where he was. What he had done was for her own good. But the tightness in his chest was back.

At last she swallowed and said, "You're the fool, Garth Whitelaw, to throw away an offer of love. You're going to end up a bitter, lonely old man.

"But I thank you for making me see that giving my love to a man like you, a man who can't—or won't—give love in return, would be like standing in front of a Brahma bull, waiting to get stomped. I know when it's time to make a break for the fence. Believe me when I say I'll be glad to put some distance between us!"

She turned and marched from the room, shoulders back, head held high with a dignity and courage he couldn't help but admire.

He hadn't seen Candice Baylor again before she left Hawk's Way or at any time since that night. Until now. Here she was headed straight toward him, a friendly smile on her face as though that night had never happened. At least they were on neutral territory at the fairgrounds in Amarillo. It was doubtful she planned to make a scene in a public place, although that had happened to him once or twice in the past with other women. His lips flattened in displeasure as he recalled such a moment.

"Hello, Garth."

He had forgotten how husky her voice was. The sound rasped over his flesh, lifting the hairs. He didn't know what to say, so he said nothing. An awkward silence followed. Candy was close enough that he could smell the perfume she was wearing, the light scent of lilacs. He felt his body tightening in instant response to her allure and swore under his breath.

She froze and her face paled.

Garth clamped his back teeth and stood in silence.

"I need to talk to you," she said at last.

"If you want to buy a horse, see the auctioneer."

"Not about that."

Garth refused to help her by asking what she wanted. He watched the expressions chase across her face. Frustration, then anger, then determination.

"I'd like you to join me for a drink at the hotel across the street," she said.

"I didn't think you were old enough to drink in a public place."

She flushed painfully, but her chin came up a notch. "I'm not. I'll have a glass of tea. I have a proposal I'd like to make to you. I thought we might as well get away from the noise and bustle of the sale. Will you join me?"

Garth listened to the auctioneer's patter over the microphone and the sounds of horses neighing. People were going right on with their lives, unaware that he was being confronted by a specter from his past.

He knew it would be a mistake to go with her. Despite the three years that had passed since he had seen Candy Baylor, he was still attracted to her. She was definitely not a child anymore. Her voice, her face, her body had all matured. She was a woman now.

And probably not a virgin anymore.

He tried not to think about that, but couldn't get the idea out of his head. He would never have taken her innocence, but now that she was an experienced woman, why not have her? He wondered if she would be willing. His lip curled cynically. Why else had she sought him out? Probably she was taking him up on his offer to come back when she was ready to have an adult relationship with him. He sure as hell wasn't going to turn her down.

"I don't have much time," he began. He watched her face closely and saw the disappointment she couldn't hide. "But I can spare you a few minutes."

The smile was back, and a brightness in her light gray eyes that made his gut twist. He wanted her.

His mouth was so dry it was hard to swallow. His body felt taut, stretched on a rack of desire.

It was a damn good thing they were having a drink at the hotel, he thought. At least that way it wasn't far to the nearest bed.

Two

Candice Baylor wanted one thing from Garth Whitelaw—and it wasn't sex. That was a good thing, because from the look on his face as she had approached him, he wasn't the least bit happy to see her.

Her last encounter with Garth had cured her of her childish infatuation with the wrangler, but even so she couldn't help admiring the man. He stood well over six feet tall, and his lithe body was all muscle and sinew. He moved with the easy grace of someone who has spent his life depending on the strength and coordination of his body.

Over the years since that night in the parlor at Hawk's Way, Candy had tried to figure out what it was about Garth Whitelaw that had caused her to fall in love with him. She had watched him with the horses he bred and trained and seen that he was capable of gentleness, infinite patience and compassion. Her only mistake had been in thinking that Garth would be able to transfer those emotions to human beings. He had turned out to be a hard, harsh and unforgiving man where women were concerned.

As they headed toward Garth's pickup truck for the ride to the hotel, Candy stole glances at the man she had once thought she loved. His face wasn't conventionally attractive. It was full of hard planes and gaunt hollows. His dark brown eyes were feral, almost dangerous. He wore his black hair too long, down over his collar, and even his tan Western suit didn't make him look the least bit civilized.

His expression was brooding, his eyes hooded, his body taut with what Candy recognized as the first signs of desire. She felt a shiver run down her spine, aware of a sexual attraction to the rugged horseman which she thought had been put to rest forever.

Candy was grateful that the hotel was so close, since neither of them said anything to break the uncomfortable silence that had fallen between them in the truck. Once in the hotel restaurant, Garth took charge of ordering an iced tea for her and a whiskey for himself.

Candy didn't want to be interrupted when she told Garth what she wanted from him, so while they waited for their drinks to arrive, she asked about his family, whom she had met during her ill-fated visit three years before.

"Jesse and Tate are both married and have children," Garth said. "Faron..." He frowned and finished in a voice that didn't invite further probing, "Faron's gone to Wyoming on business."

"So you're all alone at the ranch now?"

"Except for Charlie One Horse."

"How is he?"

"As cantankerous as ever."

Candy knew Garth wasn't married, but she wanted to ask if he had a steady girlfriend. She resisted the impulse. It would bring back too many memories she wanted to forget. But she couldn't think of anything else to ask, either.

Fortunately, Garth picked up the slack. "I heard your father's big black stud won another cutting horse futurity."

Candy smiled. "You mean Comanche Moon? That horse can stop on a dime and give you nine cents change," she said proudly. "There's a good chance he'll be World Champion Cutting Horse this year. Not that it'll be easy to beat Hawk's

Honor. I know your stallion has proved he's a champion the past two years, but this year the title belongs to Comanche Moon."

"Any chance your father would let me buy him?"

Candy shook her head. "Comanche Moon isn't for sale. Dad wouldn't part with him for all the oil in Texas."

The waiter arrived with their drinks, and Candy fiddled with her tea, squeezing in lemon and stirring in sweetener to postpone the moment when she would have to make her proposal to the wrangler.

"All right," Garth said after he had taken a drink of whiskey. "Spit it out. What do you want?"

"I want to hire you to teach me everything you know about breeding and training cutting horses." She rushed on before he could interrupt. "If I want to be the best—and I do—I figure I need to learn from the best. That's you. As a rider, you've won every cutting horse competition there is. As a breeder, your horses have what it takes to win championships."

Garth was stunned by Candy's suggestion. It was a far cry from the sexual invitation he had been expecting. He was surprised at the sharp disappointment he felt that she wasn't seeking him out for more personal reasons. On the other hand, he was flattered by her obvious admiration for what he had accomplished with cutting horses. He was tempted to say he would take her on and teach her what he knew.

Two things stopped him. First, having her around would be a constant distraction from his work. There was no denying the way his body reacted to her. He wanted her, wanted to be deep inside her. If she came to Hawk's Way he would have her.

However, having her wasn't the problem. It was getting her to leave when he was tired of her. It was bound to get awkward if she stuck around to learn about cutting horses long after he had lost interest in having her in his bed. It never occurred to him that his interest in her wouldn't wane. No woman had ever held his attention for long after he had bedded her.

His second reason for refusing her was equally compelling. In Garth's experience, rich people thought they could buy anything with money. His mother, for one, had been tempted into an affair by the gifts of jewels and money a wealthy man had offered her. Garth Whitelaw wasn't about to hire himself out to anybody—especially not to some spoiled little rich girl.

Garth had been staring into his drink while he thought. Now he looked up and saw that Candy had caught her lower lip in her teeth. His belly tightened as he remembered the sweet taste of her. His voice grated with need when he spoke.

"I'm not interested. You go on back to college in the fall and finish your education."

Her eyes flashed with irritation, but her voice remained calm. "In the first place, I've graduated college. I went straight through and finished early. In the second place, I'm prepared to pay—"

"Keep your money, sweetheart. Now, if you'd like to make me a different proposition..." He let his voice trail off suggestively.

"Like what?" she asked hesitantly.

"Seems to me we have some unfinished business together."

Candy realized suddenly what Garth wanted from her. She felt the heat skating up her throat. She had hoped and prayed he had forgotten her youthful indiscretion. Here it was, back to haunt her. "I'm only interested in a business relationship, Garth. If you're worried about me making any other overtures, you can relax. I wouldn't dream of imposing myself on you."

"Unfortunately, I can't make the same promise. I find you a damned attractive woman. Now that you're not a virgin anymore, I can't guarantee I could keep my hands off you."

Candy opened her mouth to tell him "I am too a virgin!" and snapped it shut again. It would be too embarrassing to discuss such a thing, and he was bound to say something that would make her so furious she wouldn't be able to talk.

"What if I made it clear I didn't want anything to do with you?" she asked.

"I've never forced myself on a woman," Garth said. "I've never needed to." His smile was slow in coming, but no less devastating to her senses.

Candy pressed her thighs together, but that did nothing to stop the growing warmth between her legs. She was still determined to get what she wanted, even if it meant she would have to deal with Garth's sexual overtures. She could handle him. Especially since he had promised no force would be involved.

"Look," she said, "I'm willing to work with you on a purely professional basis if you'll just work with me."

"That's the point, sweetheart. I don't want to work with you."

Candy gritted her teeth to keep from snapping something back at Garth that would forever close the door to Hawk's Way. "I'll give you some time to think about it and—"

"I don't need time to think," Garth interrupted. "The answer is no. Not now, not ever."

"You are the most stubborn, most arrogant sonofa—"

Garth's eyes narrowed. "I think you've said enough."

There was something in his tone of voice that warned Candy he was at the end of his rope. One look at his face told her that words weren't going to change his mind. She hid her disappointment, not wanting to give him something else to throw back in her face. "All right, Garth. If that's the way you feel, I suppose I'll have to look elsewhere for someone to teach me what I want to know."

Garth wondered who she would find. Sam Longstreet at the Double Bar Ranch was good. He was a bachelor, too. Garth felt a sudden unreasonable jealousy, but forced it down. He stood when Candy did and reached out a hand to help her from the booth.

Candy slid out on her own. Her eyes met Garth's one last time, searching for any sign that he might relent. When she found none, she said, "Goodbye, Garth." Then she turned and walked away.

Garth stared after her, wondering if he had done the right thing. He sat back down and finished off his whiskey. Then, because he was beginning to think maybe he had been too hasty, he ordered another drink and nursed it while he tried to get the image of Candice Baylor out of his mind.

Meanwhile, Candy headed upstairs to the hotel suite she shared with her father. She was glad he wasn't there, because by the time she arrived, she was on the verge of tears. Candy hadn't admitted to herself how much she had been counting on

Garth Whitelaw to agree to her plan. She had tied up her hopes and dreams for the future in that one request. And it had been denied.

Candy slipped into her bedroom and closed the door behind her. She felt weary beyond words. She lay down on the bed and hugged a pillow to her chest, pressing it to her mouth to hold back the sobs that threatened.

It was dark when Candy's father knocked on her door.

"Candy? I've been waiting downstairs for you. I thought we were supposed to have supper together. Are you all right, honey?"

"I'm fine, Daddy." Candy quickly turned on a lamp and swiped at her eyes, which were red from all the crying she had done.

"Can I come in?" he asked.

She jumped up and crossed to the bathroom for a damp cloth. She dabbed at her eyes, trying to undo the ravages her tears had left. "Come on in, Daddy."

When she came out of the bathroom, her father took one look at her and said, "What happened? What's wrong?"

"It shows, huh?"

He opened his arms and Candy crossed into them. With her father's arms around her she confessed what she had wanted to do and Garth's rejection of her proposal. Of course, she didn't mention anything about Garth's personal interest in her. Evan Baylor was very protective of his daughter and would likely make things worse by confronting the younger man.

"It doesn't matter, Daddy," she finished. "I suppose it was pretty presumptuous to think he'd be willing to teach me. I'll find somebody else."

"But Garth Whitelaw is the best!" Evan protested.

Candy shrugged and managed a smile. "Then I guess I'll have to take second best."

Evan's mouth firmed. He hadn't started out as one of the richest men in Texas, and he had learned over the years how to get what he wanted. What he wanted now was to take that look of defeat and despair off his daughter's face. Which meant he had to find a way to get Garth Whitelaw to reverse his decision.

"Don't you worry, honey," Evan said. "Maybe when Garth thinks it over he'll change his mind."

"He sounded pretty definite about his decision," Candy said.

Evan didn't bother arguing with her. "You still hungry?"

"I'd rather have something sent up to the room, if you don't mind."

"Not at all," Evan said. That would give him a chance to hunt up Garth Whitelaw and see about changing the man's mind. "You order whatever you like. I think I'll go out and get myself a good steak. See you tomorrow morning.''

''Good night, Daddy.''

''Good night, honey.'' Evan gave his daughter a hug and received a kiss on the cheek. He adored his only child. She was the light of his life. He would do anything to see her happy. His eyes narrowed in calculation as he began to examine his options.

Evan headed back downstairs. Candy had left Garth Whitelaw in the hotel restaurant. There was just a chance the man was still there. Sure enough, as Evan entered the restaurant Garth was just on his way out. He had his arm around a luscious-looking redhead.

''Hello there, Garth,'' Evan said. ''I see you've got yourself some entertainment for the evening.''

''Yes, sir,'' Garth agreed with a grin.

''I wonder if I could take a few moments of your time before you retire. I have a proposition to make to you.''

Garth glanced down at the redhead. She wasn't the woman he wanted, as Evan Baylor's appearance reminded him.

Evan took advantage of Garth's hesitation to hand the redhead a hundred dollar bill. ''Why don't you go have yourself a drink?'' he said.

The redhead looked from Garth to Evan and smiled broadly. ''Why sure, mister. Whatever you say.''

Garth's brow arched as what he saw reinforced both his distrust of women and his belief that the rich used their money to get what they wanted. He eyed Evan warily, but when the older man gestured, he joined him in a booth in the hotel bar.

"What are you drinking?" Evan asked.

"Whiskey."

Evan held up a twenty, and a waitress quickly appeared. "Two whiskeys," he said.

Garth remained silent. He knew Evan Baylor well enough to appreciate the man's shrewd business sense. He figured Evan wanted something from him, and it wasn't too hard to guess that it might have something to do with his recent conversation with Candy.

Evan didn't wait for the whiskeys. He got right down to business. "What would it take for you to accept my daughter's proposition?"

"I'm not for sale," Garth said flatly.

"Of course not," Evan placated. "But there must be something you want that you can't get on your own. Some new piece of land to expand Hawk's Way. Some new mare. Some stud you'd like to have."

"Did Candy put you up to this?" Garth demanded.

"She doesn't know I'm here. In fact, she's willing to settle for second best. I'm not. There must be something I have that you want," Evan insisted.

Garth started to tell Evan Baylor to go to hell. Then he thought of something Evan had that he wanted very much. "Comanche Moon," he said in a soft voice.

Evan hissed in a breath. "That stud's going to be World Champion Cutting Horse this year."

"That's my price." Garth was certain the old man would never pay it. That was the only reason he had even suggested it.

"Done."

"What?"

"You teach my daughter everything you know about cutting horses, and I'll give you Comanche Moon."

"What if she quits before I've taught her what I know?" Garth knew ways to make that happen.

Evan stared down at work-roughened hands. He might be rich, but he still worked from dawn to dusk each day. And he had taught his daughter everything he believed about hard work and persistence being the roads to success.

"Candy won't quit," Evan said certainly. He looked up at Garth. "I'm so sure she won't quit that if she does, I'll give you the stud anyway."

Garth shook his head. "If she quits, I buy the stud at a fair price." He didn't want to cheat Evan, and he was pretty certain Candy Baylor wasn't going to be hanging around Hawk's Way for very long. He didn't plan to make it easy on the girl if she came to live at his ranch. He had already told her there was only one thing he wanted from her. If he didn't end up fulfilling his part of the bargain with Evan because the girl couldn't handle everything he threw at her, Garth wanted to pay for the horse.

"Done." Evan held out his hand to be shaken by the other man. He knew his daughter well. Garth Whitelaw was in for a big surprise if he thought the girl would quit.

"There's one condition," Evan said. He knew how upset Candy got when he used his money to get his own way. His daughter was just stubborn enough to refuse to go along with the bargain if she found out the truth about the deal he had made with Garth. "You can't tell my daughter that I had anything to do with your change of mind."

"That's fine with me," Garth said. After all, he had just gotten through telling Candy he couldn't be bought. He wasn't willing to admit—even to himself—that he had spent the better part of the afternoon seeking some way to get Candy Baylor alone at Hawk's Way.

"One other thing," Evan said.

"Now what?"

"I know your reputation with women," Evan said.

Garth stiffened. "What does that have to do with anything?"

"I don't want my daughter hurt."

The warning was there, and the threat also. Garth wasn't offended. He had every intention of taking Candice Baylor to bed, and no intention at all of marrying her, so he could understand her father's concern. Nevertheless, Garth didn't believe Candy was going to suffer from their relationship.

"Rest assured, your daughter won't find herself in any situation she doesn't want to be in," he said at last.

That wasn't much comfort, but Evan realized it was the only reassurance he was going to get. He had a lot of confidence in his daughter. She had managed to handle herself in some pretty tight situations. "All right," he said. "I suppose that's the most I can ask. I'll make sure Candy is downstairs for breakfast tomorrow. Say about eight o'clock?"

"I'll be there," Garth said. "Don't worry. I'll take care of making the necessary excuses for my change of mind. Your daughter won't suspect a thing."

Three

Candy stared suspiciously at Garth. Against all reason, he had joined her and her father for breakfast in the hotel dining room. Then her father had suddenly remembered an appointment and left her alone with the rancher.

"What's going on?" she demanded.

Garth shrugged. "I changed my mind."

Candy sat stunned for a moment. Then she smiled. "I'm so glad." Her face lit up with happiness, but it didn't take long for a shadow to cloud her joy. Her teeth caught her lower lip and her brow furrowed.

"What changed your mind, Garth? My father didn't—"

"I figured I'd have a better chance of getting what I want from you if I had you closer to home," Garth said.

"Oh." Candy thought about that for a moment. The roguish grin on Garth's face left little doubt what it was he really wanted from her in exchange for the knowledge she wanted from him. "I think it only fair to warn you that I'm the kind of girl who doesn't have to be burned twice to learn it's dangerous to stick your hand in the fire."

"Meaning?"

"Meaning I plan to keep my distance from you at Hawk's Way."

"That's going to be a little difficult, considering the fact we'll be working side by side every day," Garth pointed out.

Candy gave an exasperated snort. "You know what I mean."

"I'm afraid I do. Lest there be any misunderstanding, I'm agreeing to this arrangement because I want you in my bed. I'm going to do my level best while you're at Hawk's Way to convince you to join me there. Now that all the cards are on the table, do you still want to come?"

"Oh, I'm coming," Candy reassured him. "That was never in doubt. Only, as long as we're both being so honest, I think you should know that I'm cured of the love or infatuation or whatever it was I felt for you three years ago. I won't set my heart on a platter and watch you refuse it again. You're welcome to do your best to seduce me. But I'd never have sex with a man I didn't love. If you're smart, you won't waste your time trying."

"It's my time." Garth was irritated, infuriated and not sure why. He didn't want her love. Why the hell would she think he cared whether she offered it to him? All he wanted was the pleasure two consenting adults could enjoy in bed together. Candy's opposition only increased his desire for her and made the chase that much more interesting. She would give in sooner or later. He had never met a woman yet who hadn't.

"I'll expect you at Hawk's Way by the end of next week," he said.

"So soon?"

Garth arched a questioning brow. "Is there something you need to do before you start?"

"Not really." Candy thought of the spring charity ball she had been planning to attend in Fort Worth. She would have to call Edward Vargas and break their date. "No, no problem at all," she said. "I'll be there next Friday."

On the following Friday, Garth was on tenterhooks from the moment he woke up. He couldn't sit still for breakfast, and Charlie One Horse kicked

him out of the kitchen when he complained about
the coffee.

"Get out of here and go to work," Charlie ordered. "Either that filly'll show up or she won't.
Worryin' about it ain't goin' to change anythin'."

Garth saddled up a three-year-old quarter horse
and began working him in the corral. A cutting
horse was bred and trained to separate a cow from
the herd and keep it from rejoining the other animals.

In olden days, as now, cutting cattle from the
herd was a necessary function in order to brand
animals or to dose them with medicine. Garth had
the satisfaction of knowing that the sport for which
he trained his horses also had a utilitarian purpose. Some horses were suited for the sport and
thrived on the competition. Others didn't. The
ability to stop and turn on a dime was of ultimate
importance if the horse was going to be able to keep
ahead of the cow.

Garth put the three-year-old through his paces,
making sure to stop and back the horse at each turn
so the animal kept his weight on his heels, giving his
front end mobility. He gripped the saddle horn and
hung on, giving commands with his knees while the
horse leaped, dodged and wheeled with breathtak-
ing speed to keep the cow at bay.

Garth was concentrating hard on what he was
doing. It wasn't until he gave his horse a pat on the

neck at the end of the workout that he realized Candy had been standing with her arms folded over the top rail of the corral watching him.

"He's wonderful!" she said.

"He needs more work," Garth countered.

Candy bit back the compliment she had been about to make about Garth's riding, certain he would only contradict her about that, as well.

Garth kneed the stallion toward Candy as she slipped through the wooden bars and approached him. When Garth stepped down from the saddle, Candy ran her hands knowingly over the quarter horse checking his conformation. She looked to see whether he had low hocks that could handle the abrupt stops, slides and pivots required of a cutting horse.

"He's a beauty," she said. "What's his name?"

"Stop and Go."

Candy grinned. "That certainly fits." She followed Garth as he led the horse into the barn to unsaddle him. "What were you teaching him today?"

"The basics," Garth said, unconsciously beginning the lessons he had promised to teach. "Traveling with the cow. Stopping, collecting, and moving his front end to stay with the cow."

Garth led the horse into one of the stalls. Candy closed the door behind him, then stood on the bottom rail and leaned over to watch while Garth un-saddled the animal.

"I noticed Stop and Go works with his head up. Does that slow him down?" she asked.

Garth shook his head. "All horses are different. Some work with their heads up, some down. What's most important is the stop that sets up the turn." Garth temporarily set the saddle on the side of the stall, slipped off the bridle and replaced it with a halter.

Candy stepped down off the stall door and opened it as Garth came back through with the sweaty horse.

"You can take him out back and hose him off now," Garth said.

Candy opened her mouth to say that bathing horses wasn't what she had come to learn but shut it again. She had made up her mind to follow directions and do what she was told. That way there was less chance of a confrontation with Garth.

A look down at what she was wearing made Candy grimace. The designer jeans, red silk shirt and matching red boots she had worn to travel in were a little fancy for hosing down horses. "Can you give me a minute to change?"

"Never mind. I'll do it myself."

Garth was being totally unreasonable, but Candy wasn't about to give him the opportunity to say later that she cared more about her clothes than the job. "Give him to me," she said. "I'll take care of him."

Candy accidentally brushed the crisp hairs across the back of Garth's hand as she took the lead rope from him. It felt as though she had been zapped with an electrical shock. She stared at the wrangler with a stricken expression.

Before she even considered asking Garth to teach her about cutting horses, Candy had convinced herself she was over her infatuation with the wrangler. Her reaction to the mere touch of his hand was a shock—both literally and figuratively.

Candy had believed herself no longer susceptible to Garth's powerful animal magnetism. Since she had firmly quashed the strong emotional feelings of three years ago, she had figured there was not much the cowboy could do to entice her into his bed. Thus, she was confounded by the surge of sexual excitement she had just experienced.

Candy stood frozen for a second, staring at the spot where she had touched Garth. For the sake of the horse, she forced herself to move slowly rather than jerking her hand away. But once she and Garth were no longer touching, she quickly headed out the back door of the stable.

"Don't get too wet," he called after her.

Candy shot him a look over her shoulder. "Don't worry, Boss. I won't melt." In fact, a dousing with cold water might be just what she needed to cool off.

As Garth watched the sway of two rear ends moving away from him, it suddenly dawned on him how quickly and easily Candy had insinuated herself into his workday.

One thing Garth hadn't considered when he told Candy he would teach her was whether she would be an apt pupil. It appeared that she was serious about learning the art of breeding and training cutting horses. Which added an entirely different dimension to their relationship.

All Garth's plans had evolved around the physical connection he planned to have with Candy. Now he was going to have to deal with her on intellectual terms, as well. He smiled wryly. That was certainly going to be a first for him. He had always kept business and pleasure separate in the past.

Garth stepped to the next stall and began saddling another horse, a two-year-old he had raised from birth. He soon found that he had certainly been right about the fact that Candy would prove a distraction. The third time he let the colt get away with turning before he made a stop, Garth ended the lesson. He didn't want the horse to end up with bad habits because his trainer's mind had strayed to some female.

Meanwhile, Candy had turned over the cooled-down quarter horse to one of the hands working in the stable and headed back to the house for a change of clothes. The silk blouse hadn't survived the encounter. The red boots would be fine to work in, but she wouldn't be dressing up in them again. She figured she better find out where Charlie One Horse had put her suitcases.

Candy stopped and stared at the place that would be her home for the next several months. She had fallen in love with Hawk's Way the first time she had seen it. The ranch house was an imposing two-story white frame structure that looked a lot like an antebellum mansion. It had four twenty-foot-high fluted columns along its face and railed first-and second-story porches that ran the length of the house. The road leading to the house was lined with magnolias, while the house itself was shaded by the branches of a moss-laden live oak.

For all its grandeur outside, the house was very much a home. The oak and pine furniture that had been passed down from generation to generation showed the hard wear of frontier life. However, though gouged and scraped, it was kept polished to a fine sheen.

Candy pulled the screen door open and entered the kitchen. "Charlie? Where are you, Charlie?" When she got no answer, she headed upstairs. She expected to find her things in the guest bedroom where she had stayed the last time she had come to

Hawk's Way. A glance inside the room showed it was bare.

Candy pursed her lips and began a search from room to room upstairs. Each room showed the personality of its former occupant, and Candy got images of Garth's siblings—independent, uncontrolled, unpredictable—as she passed from one room to another. Each step took her closer to the end of the hall, where she knew Garth slept. Sure enough, she found her suitcases in the bedroom next to his. Candy frowned.

She walked in and closed the door behind her, muttering her displeasure as she began stripping off her wet clothes. There was nothing subtle about the message Garth was sending. It was only a step or two from her bedroom to his.

Despite her anger at Garth's blatant manipulation, she had to admire the room itself. The canopy over the bed was trimmed in eyelet lace, as was the spread. The dry sink and chest were antiques, and the back of the rocker beside the bed was hand-carved. Garth had put her in a room that held a wealth of Whitelaw heritage. Candy could almost feel the love and hate, the hope and despair of the generations of Whitelaws who had slept in this room.

The view from the window took Candy's breath away. The mountainous Palo Duro Canyon area was rugged terrain that had once provided a haven for raiding Comanches. It was a landscape as harsh and unforgiving as the man who owned it.

She was just buttoning up a blue chambray shirt when the door opened.

"Candy? It's Garth. Are you in there?"

"Garth, I—" Before Candy could say she didn't have her jeans on yet, Garth opened the door. She glared at him and said, "You could have knocked."

"I'm glad I didn't." Garth found himself treated to the sight of Candy's bare legs beneath the tails of a Western shirt. "I just came up to ask whether you'd like to take a ride with me. I have to check on some stock in the north pasture."

"I'd like that." She hesitated, then said, "I want to know why I'm not staying in the same room I used the last time I was here."

"The answer to that ought to be obvious. I wanted you close to me."

Candy's fists landed on her hips. "It's not going to make any difference where you put me. I'm not going to go to bed with you."

"Then it won't matter if you stay here," Garth shot back. His eyes slid to her legs where another inch or two of flesh had been exposed when her fisted hands gathered the shirt at her waist. His heart, which was already thudding from his race upstairs in search of her, picked up a beat.

For a few hectic minutes when he couldn't find Candy anywhere around the barn, Garth had feared she had packed up and gone home. He refused to admit how relieved he was to discover her here. He let his eyes feast on the sight of her.

"If you're through ogling, I'd like to finish getting dressed," Candy said.

Garth tipped his hat in acknowledgement of her demand, turned and sauntered out the door. He stopped just beyond the threshold and said, "If you're not at the barn in five minutes, I'm leaving without you."

Candy slammed the door behind him. She considered making him wait on her, then admitted he probably wouldn't. At which point she grabbed a pair of Levi's and jerked them on, tucked in her shirt and added a tooled leather belt. Then she sat down on the canopy bed, pulled on socks and stuck her feet into a pair of sturdy Western boots.

Four and a half minutes later she was standing at the door to the barn. Garth walked down the center aisle leading two saddled horses. He handed the reins of a bay gelding with four white stockings to Candy and led a coal black stallion out of the barn for himself.

Candy checked the length of the stirrups and the cinch to make sure it was tight. Then she mounted and followed Garth down a dirt road that led to the north pasture. She was pleased to note that Garth had put her on a spirited animal, but she felt self-conscious as the wrangler evaluated her seat on the horse. She forced herself to relax. She had learned to ride before she could walk and had been a champion herself in several eighteen-and-under junior cutting horse futurities.

Still, she breathed a sigh of relief when Garth said, "I'm glad to see you've got an easy hand on a horse's mouth. That's one less thing I'll have to teach you."

"I'm willing to take pointers on anything you think could stand improvement," she said.

"That's good to know. Because I have a suggestion."

"Oh?" Candy tensed.

"Relax. I'm not going to bite you. At least, not anytime soon."

Candy laughed. "Be careful. I might bite back." She made the mistake of looking at Garth and saw the sudden leap of desire in his eyes. "Forget I said that," she muttered.

Fortunately they had reached the pasture where several mares and their foals were grazing along with some stock that was still too young to be ridden. Candy dismounted and, following Garth's lead, tied her horse to the closest fence post. Garth's stallion whinnied at the mares, who looked up and then went back to grazing again. Candy wished she could be so nonchalant when Garth demanded her attention.

She assessed the quarter horse mares and realized she was seeing the best of the best. She whistled her appreciation. To her surprise, one of the yearling colts began trotting toward her. Then she realized Garth had slipped through the fence and was holding an apple in his palm, waiting for the colt to approach.

After sidestepping and tossing his head several times, the yearling walked over to Garth and took the apple from him. As the chestnut-colored colt stood there munching, Garth handled the animal, running his hands over its neck and chest, down over the withers and back to the hindquarters, then down the legs and up again.

"Come here," he said to Candy in a quiet voice.

Candy joined him, and he began another lesson. He stepped behind her, took her hand in his and made the same journey as before. Only this time, his hand moved hers across the colt's sleek coat, pointing out the yearling's good and bad points for her edification.

At last he moved to the colt's head. "He's short between the eye and muzzle, has a wide forehead, a nicely defined jowl and a straight profile. His eyes are wide-set, and his ears are set forward and close to each other. Damn near perfect."

Garth let go of Candy's hand at last, but he didn't step back. Their bodies were aligned so that each could feel the other's heat. Candy forced herself to focus on the horse, not the man standing behind her. She scratched the blaze on the colt's face and said; "You didn't comment on the way his neck meets his shoulder."

Garth had his right hand on the colt's withers and reached past her with his left to run a hand down the colt's neck, effectively trapping her between his arms. "It might be a bit low, but not enough to make a difference," he said at last.

Candy felt Garth's moist breath against her cheek when he spoke. She turned slightly and realized that their mouths were only inches apart. She raised her eyes to his and saw they were hooded, the dark eyes lambent. She was appalled at the desire that pooled between her legs. Her breasts felt full and achy. Her nipples were erect.

Candy stood frozen as Garth lowered his mouth to hers. She was prepared for violence. It was what she expected, and it would have freed her from his thrall. His lips barely touched hers before they retreated, only to return for another taste. She kept her mouth closed, but he made love to her lips, kissing first one edge and then the other of her mouth before sliding his tongue along the seam.

Candy moaned when she felt Garth's tongue slip between her lips. The warmth, the wetness, made her feel weak. She needn't have worried about falling. Garth's hand slid around her waist and turned her to face him, sealing their bodies together from the waist down. There was no mistaking his arousal, which only intensified her own disjointed feelings.

Candy pressed the heels of her hands against Garth's chest with the thought of pushing him away, but instead her fingers curled into his cotton shirt, clutching him tight.

Candy was in way over her head. She knew how sexually experienced Garth was, and that she had to guard against his persuasiveness. But it was that experience which made him so successful in his seduction. Whenever she seemed reluctant for him to go a step further, he backed off. So a love bite on her throat that drew a guttural groan from her was followed by teasing kisses that had her melting in his arms.

His fingers tunneled into her hair and held her still for a ravishing kiss, then slid down to her nape and gently massaged the tender flesh there.

Candy was far more innocent than Garth knew. Her disastrous experience with him three years ago had kept her from letting things get very far with the men she had dated in college. No man besides Garth had ever touched her.

So when Garth's hand slid up to cup her breast, it recalled the memory of how he had hurt her in the past. She cried out in anticipation of the pain and jerked herself from his grasp. Her cry frightened the colt, which turned and kicked up its heels.

Garth grabbed her and threw them both out of the way of the colt's slashing hooves. He took the brunt of the fall, protecting her in his arms. When they finished rolling, he was lying on top of her in the grass.

Candy stared up at him, eyes wide with fright.

"You damn fool! Don't you know better than to shout like that around a horse?" Garth said between gritted teeth.

"I was—"

"What were you yelling for, anyway? I know damn well I didn't hurt you!" he ranted.

"Not *this* time," Candy retorted.

She watched a muscle work in Garth's jaw, but his tirade abruptly ended. She gave his shoulders a push. "You can get off me now."

Garth took most of his weight off her, but he didn't free her. The grass was surprisingly cool beneath her, and several blades tickled the back of her neck. She closed her eyes and turned her face away, unable to bear the taunting look on his face. But he didn't allow her to hide from him for long. He grasped her chin and turned her face toward him.

"Open your eyes, Candy."

"No, Garth."

He lowered his body so that he was cradled between her thighs. He was aroused again. Or still. Candy didn't know which, but it hardly mattered.

"Open your eyes," he demanded.

She blinked against the sun's glare and stared at him in defiance. "Let me up."

"In a minute. First, we have a few things to get settled."

"I don't want to hear anything you have to say."

"That's too damn bad," Garth said. "I think what just happened between us proves you're not indifferent to me."

Candy's lips pressed flat. She couldn't deny the rush of passion she had felt in Garth's arms. Or the fact that she had enjoyed every moment of his kisses. But she still wasn't sophisticated enough to accept the fact that she could feel sexual desire for a man she wasn't even sure she liked.

When she remained stubbornly silent, Garth commanded, "Talk to me, Candy."

"What do you want me to say? That I enjoyed what happened? I did. That I want to repeat the experience? I don't! You're pushing too far, too fast, Garth."

Garth eased his body away from hers. Her outburst was something he understood. A woman liked a little courting before she succumbed to a man. He was willing to play the game, now that Candy had told him the rules. "Sure, sweetheart. Whatever you say."

Garth rose and pulled Candy to her feet. He began dusting her off, but she slapped his hands away. "Leave me alone. I can take care of myself."

She swatted the last of the grass from her fanny, then turned back around to face Garth. "What are you grinning at?"

"Can't a man smile when he's happy?"

Candy scowled. She marched past Garth toward where she had left the gelding tied and heard Garth following close behind her. She felt the heat of him, smelled the musky scent of aroused male that even three years later had the power to make her remember the taste of him. Candy turned, forcing Garth to stop in his tracks.

She jabbed a finger at his chest and said, "Don't push me, Garth. You won't like what I'll do."

Garth's grin widened. "Try me."

Pushed to the limit, Candy took him at his word. Her hand arced and her open palm hit his cheek with a loud crack. She was appalled at the clear imprint of her hand on his face and the dark flush that quickly followed. Garth's eyes narrowed, and his lips flattened, but he made no move to retaliate.

Candy trembled, shaken by the attack, which had surprised her as much as it had Garth. She swallowed over the sudden thickness in her throat. "I . . . I didn't mean . . ."

"Forget it," Garth snapped. "We'd better be getting back to the house. Charlie will have supper waiting for us."

Candy mounted her horse and rode back to the ranch house in silence. She couldn't imagine what had caused her to react so violently to Garth's provocation. She had never hit anyone before in her life.

When the ranch house came into sight, Candy realized that if she didn't want to have to apologize in front of Charlie One Horse she had better do it now. "I'm sorry."

Garth eyed her askance. "It's not the first time I've been slapped."

Candy flushed. "It's the first time *I've* slapped someone," she retorted. "Are you going to accept my apology, or not?"

"Apology accepted."

As they dismounted at the stable, Candy had the awful feeling that Garth wasn't the sort of man who easily forgave and forgot. She was bound to him and Hawk's Way for the next several months, at least until she had learned enough to feel confident about opening her own stable. Now they were engaged in a war of nerves. He was determined to have her; she was determined to resist him.

Candy had been certain she could hold her own against any efforts Garth made to seduce her. As she had just discovered, things weren't turning out quite like she had planned. She made up her mind that she, for one, wasn't going to be the next tempting morsel on Garth Whitelaw's plate. Because as she knew from bitter experience, the wrangler ate up little rich girls, and spit them out when he was done.

Four

——

Charlie One Horse was bent over, checking the pot roast in the oven, when Candy came through the kitchen on her way upstairs. She mumbled something about washing up and disappeared in the direction of the stairs. Charlie took one look at Garth's face as he stepped through the screen door and poured him a whiskey from the bottle he kept over the stove. "What you been doin' to that girl got her so mad she whacked you?"

Garth rubbed his cheek, wondering how Charlie knew he had been slapped. To his chagrin, he felt several scratches left by Candy's nails. "Stay out of it, Charlie." Garth sat down at the heavy oak table in the center of the kitchen. He downed the finger of whiskey and held out his glass for another.

"She ain't like them other women of yours," Charlie said as he poured the second whiskey.

"Candy knew what she was getting into when she agreed to come here," Garth said. "Let it go, Charlie. This is none of your business."

"Ain't nothin' ever my business, but I'm the one gotta put up with your bad temper when some female's givin' you fits."

"Charlie." Garth's voice held a warning tone that made the housekeeper look behind him. Candy was standing in the kitchen doorway.

"Are we eating in here?" she asked.

"You can forget the silver and crystal," Garth said. "You're not a guest at Hawk's Way anymore."

Candy stuck her hands in the pockets of her jeans to hide her agitation. "I wasn't expecting any special treatment. I was just asking where supper is being served."

"I'm afraid I have to disappoint you there, too," Garth said. "The food's on the stove. Every man helps himself."

Charlie shot Garth an incredulous look. That was the first he had heard of such a practice. When the family was home they ate supper in the dining room. Charlie usually served the meal, although Tate or Faron sometimes took a turn.

Charlie picked up a pair of pot holders, took the pot roast out of the oven and plopped it on top of the stove. He looked pointedly at Garth. "Here it is. Dig in."

Garth gave Charlie a baleful stare which the old man ignored.

Charlie took out two plates and filled them with roast beef, potatoes and carrots. He handed one plate to Candy and took the other for himself, then made sure they had silverware and glasses of tea. He settled on a chair on the opposite side of the table from Garth and pulled out a chair next to him for Candy.

"Delicious," Candy said as she dug in. "You really are a good cook, Charlie."

"Thanks, girl."

Garth was torn between his hunger and his pride. Finally he got up and served himself a plate of food. "We'll start work at dawn tomorrow," he said to Candy. "You might as well learn how and what we feed our stock."

"Don't you hire people to take care of that sort of thing?" Candy asked.

"Sure," Garth said. "But somebody has to tell them what to do. Parasite prevention, fresh water, proteins, vitamins and minerals and the right amount of forage are all as important as the right amount and kind of feed."

Candy felt a little overwhelmed. "Am I going to learn all that?"

"That's up to you. But it's as true of horses as it is of humans—you are what you eat. If you want healthy animals, you have to pay attention to nutrition."

Candy nodded her head in understanding. "I see what you mean. All right. Is there some sort of literature that explains all that?"

Charlie exchanged a look with Garth. Apparently there was more to the spoiled little rich girl than met the eye.

Garth had known Candy was clever. Now she had proved she was also inquisitive, which was not a bad trait for a pupil. "Sure," he said. "I've got lots of stuff you can read. If you come into the parlor with me after supper—"

Candy nearly choked on a bite of food. Charlie slapped her on the back, but it took a moment for her to stop coughing. She wasn't about to follow that beast back into his den anytime soon.

Garth swore under his breath when he realized that Candy's memory of their encounter three years ago was as vivid as his own. He stood, leaving his food half finished. "I'll put the books on my desk. You can get them on your way upstairs later. I'm going out."

"Where you goin'?" Charlie asked. "You gotta be up early in the mornin'."

"None of your business," Garth snapped. He grabbed his hat from the rack by the back door and slapped it on his head, letting the screen door slam behind him. Then he turned right back around and stomped back through the kitchen into the parlor. They could hear books dropping on his desk. A moment later he returned. "Don't stay up late reading," he snarled. Then he was gone.

"Wonder what got into him," Charlie muttered.

Candy wasn't about to explain. She was grateful for Garth's willingness to provide the books, which led her to believe that even if he intended to pursue her, he also intended to uphold his end of the bargain.

She stayed in the kitchen long enough to help Charlie with the dishes, even though the old man said he could manage. "Things are easier when there's another pair of helping hands," Candy said as she scraped the remains of Garth's supper into the disposal.

Charlie handed her his plate and said, "I didn't think rich folks did their own dishes."

Candy smiled wryly. "My father raised me to believe in the work ethic. If he spoiled me, it was by making me believe that I could have anything I wanted if I was willing to work hard enough for it."

"So why you want to go into the horse-raisin' business?" Charlie asked.

"There's a lot of history and tradition involved with cutting horses. I want to be a part of it."

"You got all the money a gal would ever need. Why not just buy up a ranch and let somebody else manage it for you?"

"I want the satisfaction of breeding my own horses and training them to be champions. That's why I came here." She refused to admit to any other reason than her stated one, even to herself.

"Then you better get on out of here and get to those books," Charlie said. "I'll finish up."

Candy didn't want to leave, but she found herself unable to fight both Charlie and the desire to dig into the materials Garth had left for her on his desk.

It felt strange stepping into the parlor. Looking back, she wondered where she had gotten the courage to confront Garth Whitelaw and tell him she loved him. She felt extreme embarrassment— and a great sense of loss—when she looked back on that evening.

The fireplace was as cold now as it had been that long-ago night, no more than a blackened hearth. She walked up to the mantel, above which hung a map that delineated the vast borders of Hawk's Way past and present. Someday she would have a place of her own, and in the years to come her children and grandchildren would be able to point back to the moment when she had taken that first step.

Candy crossed to the rolltop desk where White-law business had been conducted over the past hundred years. There sat a stack of books and pamphlets nearly a foot high. She picked up the one on top and read: *Horse Feeding and Management.* And another: *Rules of Thumb for Equine Feeding.* And another: *Feed a Horse Like a Horse.* She thumbed through a thick book as she crossed to the leather chair by the fireplace. She turned on the standing lamp beside the chair, sat down and put her feet up on the rawhide stool at its foot and began to read.

Garth was calling himself seven kinds of a fool for leaving the comfort of his home to drive around in his pickup. He hadn't had any specific destination in mind when he had left, only the desperate need to escape. So naturally he found an excuse not to go anyplace when all he really wanted to do was return home. Near midnight Garth decided that Candy must surely be in bed, and he would have the parlor to himself for a drink, which he sorely needed.

Because Garth believed everyone to be asleep, he entered the house quietly. He headed straight for the parlor, but was brought up short when he realized there was still a light on in the room. He crossed the threshold with matching amounts of reluctance and eagerness, afraid of what he might find.

She was there.

Candy was sound asleep, stretched out in his chair. One bare foot rested on the rawhide stool. The other was draped over the arm of the chair. Her boots were strewn like fallen soldiers beside the stool. A book lay open across her stomach, and her cheek rested on her hand on the arm of the chair.

She looked young and vulnerable, and he felt a sudden anger that she should be there waiting for him. He approached her like a wolf drawn by the bait, but wary of the steel jaws of the trap waiting to snap shut on him.

He knelt beside the chair and softly called her name. "Candy."

She made a sound in her throat which he took to be a subconscious acknowledgment of his presence, but otherwise she didn't move.

He knew he should wake her up and send her to bed, but he couldn't resist the opportunity to look at her at his leisure. He had never before noticed the tiny wisps of hair at her temples or the mole just below her ear or the slight jut of her chin. Her lashes created a feathery coal crescent along cheeks that bore the tiniest of freckles. The fingernails that had scratched him were her own, cut short and covered with a clear polish.

He ran a finger over lips that looked as sweet as strawberries. She instinctively turned her face toward his caress, much as a baby might when

nudged by a mother's breast. Garth's physical reaction was powerful and instantaneous. He bit back
the oath that sought voice. The last thing he wanted
was to wake her up so she could see him on his
knees looking every bit like he was worshiping at
her feet. Not that he was. He just found her fasci-
nating to look at.

He picked up the book on her lap, closed it and
set it on top of a stack of six or seven beside the
chair. Apparently she had done a lot of reading
while he was gone. The more he learned about
Candy Baylor the less certain he became of who she
really was. None of the growing list of adjectives he
could apply to her left him feeling the least bit satisfied. He didn't want to admire her intelligence or
her curiosity or her determination. He wanted to
enjoy a romp in bed with her.

Garth knew he could probably arouse Candy
enough while she slumbered that by the time she
was completely awake she would gladly join him in
bed. He found himself strangely reluctant to take
advantage of her that way. Which made him wonder what it was about Candy Baylor that kept him
from acting the way he normally would with any
other woman.

She wasn't the most beautiful woman he had ever
known, though she was pretty enough. Perhaps it
was the way she looked at him with those light gray
eyes of hers that caused that achy feeling in his

chest. Not that she used them to flirt with—at least, not this time around. They were clear and honest and there was nothing of the deceit he had expected—and often found—in other women.

Perhaps it was the fact that she absorbed everything he taught her like a sponge. Or that she didn't mind getting her hands dirty. Or ruining an expensive silk shirt. Or eating supper at the kitchen table when he was idiot enough to suggest that that was how they did things at Hawk's Way.

He wondered what would have happened if he had taken her up on her offer three years ago. What if he had made love to her—really made love to her—both giving and accepting the love she offered in return?

Garth felt his stomach clench and recognized the feeling as cold, stark fear. He had seen how his mother's unfaithfulness eventually destroyed his father. The old man had gotten drunk every night to forget the pain. One day he hadn't quite sobered up before he went to work and had come off a bucking horse and broken his neck. Garth had been left with the responsibility of holding both Hawk's Way and the family together.

Garth had made a vow that he would never let himself care for any woman enough that she could destroy him the way his father had been destroyed. In the years since his mother's infidelity he hadn't allowed himself to even think of a woman in terms of love.

Until he had met Candy Baylor.

Garth hadn't realized the emptiness, the loneliness he had felt over the past three years until she came back into his life. It was getting harder every day to convince himself that all he felt for her was desire.

Which made him all the more convinced that what he ought to do was get her bedded and out of his life before his feelings for her made him as vulnerable to a broken heart as his father had been.

Garth considered leaving Candy where she was. One look at the awkward angle of her neck convinced him that if he did, she wouldn't be much use to him in the morning. He slid one arm under her shoulders and scooped up her legs with the other. As he stood, she rolled down his arms and settled against his chest. Her face burrowed against him, and she said something unintelligible in her sleep.

In vain, Garth fought the feelings of possessiveness and protectiveness that rose within him. He hugged her a little closer and dropped a kiss on her forehead. "Come on, sweetheart. It's time for bed."

"Good night," she mumbled.

He carried her up the stairs and down the hall. The hardest thing he had ever done in his life was to stop at her bedroom door rather than traveling two steps farther to his own. He reached out with two fingers and dragged the spread off the bed before he laid her on it. She immediately curled into a ball on her side and murmured a sigh of satisfaction.

He would have loved to undress her, but he didn't trust his willpower that far. He pulled the spread back up over her shoulder, set the alarm clock beside the bed for 5:00 a.m. and left the room, closing the door behind him.

The next morning, the look on Candy's face was sheepish when she arrived in the kitchen for breakfast.

"Did you put me to bed?" she asked Garth.

Garth grunted his assent.

"Thank you. I guess I fell asleep. I'm sorry to be a bother."

"Next time go to bed when you're tired," he said.

Candy winced at the irritation in his voice.

"Did you learn anything?" he asked.

Candy gave him an excited recitation on equine digestion that ended with, "I had no idea all of that went on inside a horse."

Garth couldn't help smiling at her enthusiasm. She talked the whole distance to the barn and asked surprisingly astute questions as he and one of the hands, a young man named Tom Handy, fed the horses in the stable.

"Who feeds the horses in the north pasture?" she asked.

"Tom will take care of that. We've got other business to do today."

"Oh?"

"How would you like to take a turn on Stop and Go?"

Candy stared at him. "You're going to let me ride him?"

"I'd rather you started with a horse who knows what he's doing while I teach you the basics. Then I'll give you a horse of your own to bring along from scratch," Garth explained.

Candy hadn't expected to be allowed to work one of Garth's horses so soon. Although when she thought about it, how else was Garth going to teach her to train cutting horses except to put her on an animal and give her instructions about what she was doing right and wrong?

Two hours later, Candy was having second thoughts about riding, cutting horses and Garth Whitelaw, in that order.

Garth touched her constantly. All under the guise of teaching her, of course. The position of her hands, the angle of her heels, the shape of her shoulders, nothing escaped his notice. When he wasn't touching her, he was barking orders.

"When the cow goes, you go. When the cow stops, you stop. Back the horse up to reinforce the stop!"

Candy had grabbed the saddle horn and hung on, using her knees to let the horse know what she wanted from him.

"Stay down in the saddle. Push your pelvis forward. Not like that! Hold up there."

Garth marched out to her and put a hand on her rear end and a hand on her belly. "Tuck in your rear end. Sit deep in the saddle and stay with the horse's movement. Understand?"

Candy was so flustered by the feel of Garth's hands on her where no other man had ever dared put them, that she couldn't find her voice to object.

"Understand?" he demanded.

Candy nodded. "You can take your hands off me now."

Garth seemed to realize suddenly where his hands were. To Candy's chagrin he drew them away slowly, making his touch a caress. She closed her eyes and bit her lip to keep from moaning.

When she opened her eyes again, Garth was on the other side of the fence. Apparently he had recognized the danger, as well.

"Concentrate on getting the horse to travel with the cow. Keep his head aimed at the cow's shoulder."

Candy nudged Stop and Go with her knees.

"Don't pressure the cow!" Garth warned.

Candy backed the horse off slightly.

"Now you're too late!" Garth remonstrated. "Travel with the cow. Travel with the cow!"

Candy was more exhausted than Stop and Go when the training session was over, but she believed both she and the horse were doing better. She waited for a word of praise from Garth. It didn't come.

"Unsaddle him and wash him down," Garth ordered. "When you get done come back, and you can watch me with the two-year-old I'm working."

"Yes, sir, your highness," Candy muttered as she rode past Garth out of the corral.

She hadn't thought she had spoken loud enough to be heard. An instant later Garth had yanked her out of the saddle, and she was standing on the ground in front of him.

"There's no royalty around here, sweetheart. Just hard-working cowboys. If you've got a problem with that, we can finish the business between ourselves, and you can skedaddle on home."

Garth emphasized his point by pulling Candy into his arms and kissing her hard. Candy kept her teeth clenched, but he used his hands on her cheeks to force her mouth open so he could thrust his tongue inside. He wasn't gentle, and she had the feeling he wanted her to fight him.

Candy was smarter than that. She kissed him back. She slipped her tongue into his mouth and tasted him the way he had tasted her. It was a toss-up which of them was more surprised by what she had done. Desire speared through her, powerful and demanding.

She forced herself to think, rather than feel. This was a war of nerves as much as a seduction. She was determined not to succumb to the desire that demanded satisfaction. If anybody cried uncle, it wasn't going to be her.

Every place Garth touched her, she touched him back.

Shoulders. Arms. Chest. Buttocks.

Both of them were gasping when he broke the kiss at last.

"Damn you, girl! You've left that horse standing there with the sweat drying on him. Take care of him!"

Candy was furious at Garth's accusation. He was as much responsible for the horse being left unattended as she was. But she wasn't about to lose her temper and give Garth a reason either to send her packing or seduce her further. "Next time stay out of my way!" she snapped as she crossed past him.

Garth stared after Candy as she picked up the reins and led the cutting horse back around behind the barn. He was shaken by how close he had come to having her right here in the open. Never had he become aroused so quickly or so completely from a woman's touch. When he was with her he felt like he was riding the edge of a steep cliff. It wasn't going to take much more to shove him off.

Similar thoughts were running through Candy's mind. She had never understood the power of her passions. It wasn't the least bit comforting to know that all Garth had to do was touch her and she responded. From the way things had gone today, every lesson was going to be a trial.

Over the next several weeks Candy realized that she had been mistaken about her feelings for Garth. To her horror, she discovered that the infatuation she had felt for him at seventeen wasn't gone at all. It had always been there, buried somewhere beneath the embarrassment and humiliation she had suffered that evening in his arms.

Every time Garth touched her—and he touched her as often as he could find an excuse—she was forced to deal not only with her body's instant reaction to his physical presence, but the growing knowledge that her heart and mind were equally involved with the man.

Candy knew the day was coming when Garth would push her too far, and she would have to make a choice. Candy couldn't decide whether it would hurt more to make love to him when she knew he didn't love her, or to leave and know that she could never come back.

During breakfast on the Fourth of July, Charlie One Horse announced that he was spending the holiday in Amarillo where he could see the parade and the fireworks.

"You two wanta come along?" Charlie asked.

"We've got work to do," Garth answered him.

Candy laughed. "It's a holiday. Surely we can—" The fierce look in Garth's dark eyes cut her off.

Garth turned to Charlie and said, "We'll be staying here."

Charlie shrugged. "Suit yourselves."

When Candy heard Charlie's rattletrap truck heading down the magnolia-lined lane, a frisson of alarm ran down her spine. It dawned on her suddenly that the old man had provided a much-needed buffer between her and Garth. Now that buffer was gone.

The difference was immediately noticeable. There was a subtle tension between them that made the horses skittish. Stop and Go performed badly, and Candy had to bite her tongue to keep from apologizing for what wasn't her fault.

"That's enough."

Garth's order, coming as it did long before sunset, told Candy she wasn't the only one who had noticed the difference. He followed her inside and watched her with hooded eyes while she unsaddled the horse and put away the tack. Then, for the first time since she had come to Hawk's Way, Garth

joined her when she took Stop and Go out back to
rinse him off.

Naturally, with Garth watching her, Candy was
all thumbs.

"I'll do that," he volunteered.

Candy gratefully handed him the hose and was
surprised when he turned it on her.

She stared at him aghast. Water dripped from her
eyelashes, nose and chin. Her blouse was plastered
to her body. "What did you do that for?" she
spluttered.

Garth grinned. "I figured you needed to cool off,
too."

It only took Candy two seconds to reach Garth
and another two seconds to wrestle the hose in his
direction. The two of them drenched each other,
laughing over who was getting the wettest.

"We'd better go get dried off," Garth said at last.

Candy followed the direction of his gaze. She
looked down and realized he could see her bra
through her shirt. From the avid look in Garth's
eyes, she knew he was seeing more than a hint of
lace. If she could see his nipples through his soaked
shirt, she suspected her bra wasn't doing a much
better job of keeping her concealed. A flush rose
from her throat to stain her cheeks.

Candy decided that going into the house with
Garth right now wasn't such a good idea. "What

about Stop and Go? We can't leave him here like this.''

''Tom can take care of him.''

Candy froze. It was unheard of for Garth to leave an animal untended that either of them had ridden.

''Let's go,'' he said.

Garth held out his hand to Candy. There was no mistaking where he was taking her, or what he had in mind when he got there. This was it, Candy thought, the moment of truth. Should she go with him, or dig in her heels and stay where she was? It was a decision she had been dreading for weeks.

She knew there might be pain waiting for her at the end of the road. Garth had rejected her love once before. But there was no denying the strength of her feelings, then or now. When all was said and done, Candy followed her heart. She placed her hand in Garth's. When a woman was in love, there really wasn't any choice at all.

Five

Garth headed straight for the house. They were both drenched, so to avoid leaving two sets of wet tracks on the tile floor in the kitchen or on the hardwood throughout the rest of the house, he lifted Candy into his arms and headed upstairs. He didn't even hesitate when he passed her bedroom door, just continued on to his own.

Garth set her down with her back to him and put his hands on her shoulders. Whether he did it to comfort her or to keep her from fleeing she wasn't sure.

Candy had never been in Garth's room, but she looked at it now, searching for anything that would tell her about the man she loved.

The first thing she noticed was how neat it was. That didn't really surprise her. Garth was a man who liked to be in control. He would want things where he could find them.

She was glad to see the pictures of his family, his sister and brothers, in frames on the various wooden surfaces around the room. There was also a picture of an older man, whom she supposed was Garth's father. She wondered why there was no picture of his mother.

Candy found hope in the fact that family was important to Garth. It was proof that he could care for people as much as he cared about horses. Whether he could love one woman and commit himself to her for a lifetime was another matter altogether.

His room was full of antiques, pieces of Whitelaw history that had been handed down from father to son. She had never doubted that Garth valued the traditions of his family. Which made her wonder whether he had ever considered how he could pass on those traditions to another generation of Whitelaws when he had so little respect for women and no use at all for a wife.

He slept in a huge four-poster bed covered with a patterned quilt. She stared at the bed, unable to take her eyes off it.

"Candy?" His voice was low, intense, as demanding as it was challenging.

She suddenly had second thoughts about what she had come here to do. "I suppose there have been a lot of women in this bed."

"Yes, there have."

Candy's heart dropped to her feet as she thought of all the women Garth must have brought here.

"My mother, my grandmother, my great-grandmother—"

Her heart swelled with joy. So this bed was reserved for Whitelaw women. Surely the fact that he had brought her to this room, to this bed, meant he felt something special for her. And maybe, just maybe, she would be able to get him to admit those feelings.

Candy turned slowly to face Garth. In his dark eyes, whether he knew it or not, was a need so fierce it sent a shiver of anticipation running through her.

"Make love to me, Garth."

He had been in such a hurry to get them here, she expected him to be impatient. Candy wouldn't have been surprised if he had simply ripped off her clothes and taken her in a fury of desire. It was infinitely worse waiting the endless moments it took him to undo her shirt one button at a time.

The wet cotton clung to her skin as he pushed the shirt off her shoulders. Candy shrugged and tugged at the sleeves to help him rid her of the garment.

With practiced hands he unsnapped the catch of her bra and pushed it out of his way—reminding her how experienced he was and how little she knew about what was to come. She caught his wrist when he reached for the zipper of her jeans.

"Your turn," she said in a shaky voice. Candy reached up and began unbuttoning his shirt. Her fingers were trembling, so it took longer than it should have, but he didn't interfere with her efforts. At long last the buttons were free, and she reached up to shove the shirt off his shoulders. Her hands skimmed across flesh that was smooth and warm. She felt his muscles bunch beneath her fingertips in response to her touch.

Intrigued by Garth's reaction, she slid her hands across his chest, playing with the dark curls there. They formed a triangle that headed down into jeans that hung low on his hips. His belly contracted as she skimmed past it.

He grabbed her wrists with enough strength that she shot a surprised look at him. His dark eyes were hooded, his nostrils flared for the scent of her, his facial muscles taut.

"Did I do something wrong?" Candy asked.

"I want to take my time," he said. "The way you were heading, things would have been over too damn fast."

Candy shivered again, only this time from the chill caused by the air-conditioning on her damp skin.

"Come on." Garth took her hand and led her toward a large, modern bathroom attached to his bedroom. Before Candy could object he had both her and himself completely stripped. She caught one quick—and somewhat awe-inspiring—glimpse of aroused male before he propelled her into the shower and followed after her.

The warm water felt wonderful. Candy closed her eyes and luxuriated in the feel of it on her back and shoulders. Her eyes blinked open when she felt Garth's hands on her as well. Every feeling was new and exquisite, and yet it felt so right to be here with him that she welcomed each sensation.

Garth's hands slid over her breasts to her belly and then around to her buttocks. He tightened his arms around her, fitting their bodies together. There was no mistaking the hard length of him, even for someone as inexperienced as she was.

"Candy," he murmured. His mouth nuzzled against her brow as his hands slid up her back to hold her tight. "You taste sweet, girl."

Candy's flesh burned everywhere it met his. Her hands roamed over his back as she caressed him the way she had yearned to all those years ago. "Garth, I—"

Candy hesitated, uncertain whether she ought to admit she was a virgin. It didn't really matter, she reasoned. In a few more minutes she wouldn't be one anymore.

"What is it, sweetheart?"

"Shouldn't we be doing this in bed?" she asked in a husky voice.

Garth laughed, a deep, resonant sound she could feel because he was holding her so close. "I just wanted to make sure you didn't catch a chill."

This time Candy laughed. "Believe me, I'm warm now."

Garth wasted no time getting them out of the shower. He wrapped Candy in his white terry-cloth robe and dried himself with a large towel which he knotted around his waist. He picked her up again and carried her into the bedroom.

"I can walk," Candy protested.

"I know, but I like the feel of you in my arms." Garth stopped beside the bed and bent so she could reach the covers. "Get the quilt, sweetheart."

Candy reached out and pulled the patterned quilt away to reveal pristine white sheets. She froze, thinking how they would look stained with virgin's blood. She opened her mouth to tell him the truth, and he kissed her quick and hard. The ferocity of the kiss left her gasping.

A moment later she was in bed, and Garth was lying beside her. She might have wished for dark-ness, because she felt naked even with Garth's robe surrounding her. But she wouldn't have missed for anything the look in Garth's dark eyes as he reached out and spread the two halves of the robe and feasted his eyes on her.

"You're so beautiful."

Candy was overwhelmed with sensations as Garth's calloused fingertips explored her body, beginning at her collarbone and heading downward between her breasts. He circled them, teasing her nipples before trailing his hand down across her belly.

Candy's body arched upward under his caresses. She pulled the towel away from his hips so flesh met flesh. Then she grabbed hold of Garth's shoulders and held on. His dark eyes never left hers as his hands, and then his warm, wet mouth, roamed her body. She made a small sound in her throat as Garth's hand slipped down between her legs.

Instinctively she tightened her thighs to prevent his invasion.

"Relax, sweetheart. You're acting just like a—"

Candy did the first thing she could think of to distract him, so he wouldn't realize the truth. Her hand slid down his belly and encircled him. She was surprised to discover he was hard and soft all at the same time.

"Whoa, Candy! Go slow, sweetheart."

Candy had no idea what the difference was between fast and slow. But she forced herself to relax, and his hand slid between her legs.

Candy gasped at the intimate contact as he slid a finger inside her.

"You're so tight. Just like a—"

Candy could see it was going to take constant distraction to keep him from getting suspicious. She did what came naturally. She pulled his head down and kissed him to shut him up. She moaned deep in her throat when his tongue mimicked the thrust and parry of lovers truly joined.

His voice was harsh when he broke the kiss. "Dammit, Candy! I want to be inside you."

"I want you, too, Garth," she murmured breathlessly.

He spread her legs with his knees and thrust hard.

Her body resisted for a second before the barrier tore, and he sank to the hilt inside her. Candy bit her lip until it bled, but a whimper of pain escaped.

Garth muttered an oath. "A virgin! I should have known. What a fool I am!"

Candy wrapped her legs around Garth and held tight to his shoulders. "It's done now, and there's no going back. Please, Garth. Make love to me."

"I'll hurt you."

"No, you won't."

Garth knew he was making a mistake. He ought to get out while the getting was good. He hadn't asked if she was protected, he had simply assumed she was. The kind of woman he normally took to bed wasn't about to take the chance of getting pregnant. Candy had been a virgin. It was a good bet she hadn't taken any precautions to prevent pregnancy, and he sure as hell hadn't, either.

But right now he wanted her with a need that was beyond anything he had ever felt before in his life. Stopping was out of the question. If there were consequences, he would deal with them. "All right, little rich girl," he said. "You've got what you wanted. Now let's see how you handle it."

Garth moved slightly and saw her wince. "Dammit! I *am* hurting you!"

He started to withdraw, but Candy stopped him again. "It's all right, really. It's just...I'm not used to... You're so big that I—"

She flushed a bright red.

Garth chuckled. "All right, sweetheart. Let's start over again."

She arched a questioning brow. "Is that possible?"

He nudged his hips against hers, and Candy felt a spiral of desire twist inside her belly. Her breasts tingled. It appeared it was more than possible.

"I'm not in any hurry," Garth said with a grin. "Let's go back a few steps."

Candy didn't understand at first what Garth meant. Five...fifteen...thirty minutes later she was writhing with pleasure beneath him. He was still inside her, but there wasn't a spot on her body he hadn't caressed, licked, bitten, sucked or kissed.

Of course, she hadn't been idle. She had learned how to touch him in ways that pushed him close to the edge. His body was covered with a fine sheen of sweat, and she could see the strain in his face as he delayed the culmination of his own pleasure to make sure she reached the pinnacle of desire.

He seemed in no hurry. He drove her to the edge only to back off again. At last she thought she would go mad if he didn't finish what he had started.

"Now!" she insisted. "Now, Garth!"

Those were the words he had been waiting to hear. Garth thrust slow and easy at first, but Candy wouldn't allow him to be gentle. Her fingernails left crescents in his flesh as she arched under him. He slipped a hand between them and found the tiny nubbin that was so sensitive by now that it took only a bare touch to set her off.

He felt her squeezing him, the tight muscles contracting around him until he could barely stand the pleasure. It was Candy's guttural cry of delight that freed him to find his own satisfaction. His head arched back and his body tautened as he released his seed in powerful racking spasms.

As Garth relaxed his weight on top of her, Candy wrapped her arms around him. She felt good. She felt wonderful. She felt loved.

"I love you," she whispered.

She felt him stiffen immediately. He took his weight on his palms and stared down at her.

"I don't want to hear that any more now than I did three years ago," he said in a harsh voice. "That was sex, sweetheart. You asked for it, and you got it."

Candy turned her head away to hide her distress. It was impossible to speak over the lump in her throat.

Fool! Fool! You should have known he had no heart. You should have protected yourself better!

Maybe he can change. Maybe all he needs is a woman to love him just for himself and not ask anything in return.

Right! And if you believe that, I've got a spavined horse I'd like to sell you.

"I'm not asking you for anything," she managed to say.

"That's good. Because I'm not offering anything," he said. "You should have told me you'd never been with a man!"

"Would it have made any difference?"

"Damn straight! I don't make a habit of deflowering virgins!"

She smiled slightly. "But you do it so well!"

"That isn't funny!" he snarled.

Her smile widened. "Oh, I don't know. I find the idea pretty amusing."

"I could have hurt you!"

"But you didn't." She put her hands on either side of his face and forced him to look into her eyes. "You brought me a great deal of pleasure. I'm not asking for any more than that, Garth. Truly I'm not. I know you don't love me." She swallowed to try and force down the thickness in her throat. "But you enjoy making love to me. If it's what we both want, where's the harm?"

Garth knew where the harm was. The harm was that he wanted her as much now—more now—than he had before they made love. That had never happened to him. Once the chase was over, he usually tired of the woman quickly. With Candy, all she had to do was look at him, and he was hard all over again. At his age that was nothing short of miraculous.

He told himself he might as well take advantage of her while she was here. Once she learned what she needed to know to run her own stable of cutting horses she would be gone. He felt that same awful weight on his chest he had felt three years ago. He rolled onto his back and pulled her on top of him.

He tunneled his hands up into her hair and tugged her mouth down to his. He kissed her fiercely, letting her feel his anger and his frustration. Her hands soothed him as they spread across his chest and set him on fire at the same time. How was that possible?

His hands slid down her back to her buttocks. He grabbed hold, leaving fingerprints where his hands had been as he lifted her and impaled her on his shaft.

Garth sighed in satisfaction as he slid inside her. Wet. Warm. Tight. How could she be ready for him so soon? His lips twisted. Probably the same way he was ready for her. They were made for each other. Man and his mate.

His mate.

Garth denied the strength of his feelings for Candy Baylor. She was just like every other woman. She wasn't to be trusted. Give your heart to a female, and she would crush it beneath her high-heeled boots. Garth Whitelaw was never going to fall for any woman. Least of all some spoiled little rich girl.

Garth sat up and pulled Candy's legs around him. His hands tangled in her hair, and he held her captive for his kiss. His tongue searched her mouth for the sweetness that he couldn't seem to get enough of. He groaned as her tongue slipped into his mouth, tasting lips and teeth and seeking equal pleasure.

Garth took Candy to sensual heights she had never imagined as they made love through the afternoon. She reveled in his touch, and touched him in return. The loving was fierce and wild and left them both overwhelmed by tumultuous feelings that threatened an already-fragile relationship.

At last Candy lay asleep in Garth's arms, exhausted by the day's pleasures. Garth lay staring at the ceiling, appalled by how vulnerable he felt. He had never before experienced what had happened in this bedroom with Candice Baylor. He had exhausted himself and her, and still he wanted her. The truth could no longer be denied. His need for her was more than sexual. It seemed to come from deep inside.

He couldn't bear the thought of any other man ever laughing with her, holding her, loving her. His feelings were totally irrational, of course. But he knew he would kill the man who touched her. Such powerful emotions left him feeling agitated. And angry.

He shook Candy. "Wake up!"

Candy woke from a dream in which Garth had just told her he loved her, so there was a soft smile on her face as she looked up at him with sleepy eyes. "What is it, Garth?" Her hand smoothed over his chest, luxuriating in the feel of him.

Garth cursed when his body—wrung out from a day of making love to her—immediately hardened with need. He grabbed a handful of Candy's blond hair and pulled her head back at a painful angle.

"What's wrong, Garth?"

She didn't struggle, didn't swear or strike out against his strength. She lay there in his arms, looking up at him with love and concern. Garth felt that now-familiar tightening in his chest. He forced himself to ignore it. He was fighting for his life.

"I'm not the marrying kind," he said through gritted teeth. "I want one thing from you. Just one thing!" He laid her down and thrust inside her.

He cried out in an agony of pleasure as Candy arched up to receive him, welcoming him, taking all of him and asking for whatever more he had to give.

She was a witch, and he was ensorceled by her. That was the only explanation for the excruciating need he felt for this particular woman. There was no time for thinking once he was inside her, or for talking, either. He thrust and she parried, taking and giving pleasure, fast and hard and deep, until he heard her cry out and joined her in reaching a plateau of pleasure beyond any they had sought or expected to find.

As he lay panting above her, his body sweat-slick and musky from their lovemaking, he said, "So long as you're at Hawk's Way, you belong to me."

"All right, Garth."

Her demure response did little to ease Garth's anxiousness. "Anytime you want to cut and leave, it'll be fine by me."

"We have a deal," Candy said. "You promised to teach me what you know about cutting horses."

"And I will."

"Then I don't see that we have anything to argue about."

Garth stared at her suspiciously. There was something wrong with her logic, although he hadn't yet figured it out. "Just so we understand each other," Garth said. "From now on you'll sleep in here with me."

Candy snuggled closer to him. "All right, Garth."

Garth pulled her tight and closed his eyes. A few moments later, sated at long last, he slept.

Candy was wide awake.

She stared beyond Garth's shoulder to the framed picture of the older man, a man without a woman by his side. She knew some people would tell her she was tilting at windmills to even hope that she could change Garth's attitude about women—about having a wife.

But he had brought her here to the bed of his forebears, and when he had discovered her virginity he hadn't tossed her out. In fact, he had made love to her again and again. Sex was a strong lure, one women had used for aeons. Candy was not above using every source of ammunition she had to lay claim to her man.

She would love him so much he wouldn't be able to live without her. She would succeed where every other woman had failed. She would wait him out. Sooner or later Garth would have to admit that what they had done wasn't *having sex,* it was *making love.* Then he would ask her to be his wife.

She just had to make sure all that happened before she learned everything she needed to know to start her own stable. Otherwise, he might kick her out before she was ready to go. Well, Garth's deft, capable pupil might suddenly have to become all thumbs.

Six

"He's so savage! How can you hope to tame him?" Candy's eyes anxiously sought Garth's, then skipped back to the black stallion that was rearing and kicking and screaming his fury in the corral. "Is there a way to make him trust humans again?"

"It will take time. And patience. Maybe even that won't be enough. Señor Santos sent Midnight to me because none of his men could do anything with the horse."

"What made him so mean?" Candy asked.

"Probably somebody beat him once upon a time. Santos bought him at auction, but the horse had gone through three or four owners by then, so there's no telling, really.''

Candy was aghast. "Beat him! How could anyone be so cruel?''

Garth's lips pursed. ''You're living in a dreamworld if you think there aren't people out there who mistreat animals. It's too bad. Santos said if I couldn't tame that black beast he'd have to put him down.''

"Oh, no, Garth! You can't let him be killed!'' Candy grasped the wrangler's arm as though to stop him from such an action. She felt a jolt of electricity the instant she touched him. Candy stared up into Garth's dark eyes and saw that he was as aroused as she was by the simple contact. ''You can tame him. I know you can!''

''I don't have the time to waste,'' Garth said. ''Santos didn't tell me what bad shape the horse is in, or I never would have let him ship the stud here.''

''I've got the time!'' Candy said. ''I'll do it. If you'll just tell me what to do.''

Garth frowned. ''I don't know. You need to concentrate on learning what you came here to learn.''

Candy flushed with embarrassment. Garth hadn't said it aloud, but over the past week her learning curve had dipped considerably. She had

IT'S FUN! IT'S FREE!
AND IT COULD MAKE YOU A
MILLIONAIRE

If you've ever played scratch-off lottery tickets, you should be familiar with how our games work. On each of the first four tickets (numbered 1 to 4 in the upper right) there are Pink Metallic Strips to scratch off.

Using a coin, do just that—carefully scratch the PINK strips to reveal how much each ticket could be worth if it is a winning ticket. Tickets could be worth from $100.00 to $1,000,000.00 in lifetime money ($33,333.33 each year for 30 years).

Note, also, that each of your 4 tickets has a unique sweepstakes Lucky Number . . . and that's 4 chances for a **BIG WIN!**

FREE BOOKS!

At the same time you play your tickets to qualify for big prizes, you are invited to play ticket #5 to get brand-new Silhouette Desire® novels. These books have a cover price of $2.99 each, but they are yours to keep absolutely free.

There's no catch. You're under no obligation to buy anything. You don't have to make any minimum number of purchases—not even one!

The fact is thousands of readers enjoy receiving books by mail from the Silhouette Reader Service™. They like the convenience of home delivery . . . they like getting the best new novels months before they're available in bookstores . . . and they love our discount prices!

We hope that after receiving your free books you'll want to remain a subscriber. But the choice is yours—to continue or cancel, anytime at all! So why not take us up on our invitation, with no risk of any kind. You'll be glad you did!

PLUS A FREE GIFT!

One more thing, when you accept the free book(s) on ticket #5, you are also entitled to play ticket #6, which is GOOD FOR A GREAT GIFT! Like the book(s), this gift is totally free and yours to keep as thanks for giving our Reader Service a try!

So scratch off the PINK STRIPS on all your BIG WIN tickets and send for everything today! You've got nothing to lose and everything to gain!

Here are your **BIG WIN Game Tickets** potentially
worth from **$100.00 to $1,000,000.00** each.
Scratch off the PINK METALLIC STRIP on each of your
Sweepstakes tickets to see what you could win and
mail your entry right away. (SEE OFFICIAL RULES IN
BACK OF BOOK FOR DETAILS!)

This could be your lucky day—GOOD LUCK!

THE BIG WIN

TICKET 1
Scratch PINK METALLIC STRIP to reveal potential value of this ticket if it is a winning ticket. Return all game tickets intact.

LUCKY NUMBER

1M 794654

TICKET 2
Scratch PINK METALLIC STRIP to reveal potential value of this ticket if it is a winning ticket. Return all game tickets intact.

LUCKY NUMBER

4U 902251

TICKET 3
Scratch PINK METALLIC STRIP to reveal potential value of this ticket if it is a winning ticket. Return all game tickets intact.

LUCKY NUMBER

3N 782429

TICKET 4
Scratch PINK METALLIC STRIP to reveal potential value of this ticket if it is a winning ticket. Return all game tickets intact.

LUCKY NUMBER

9Q 788102

FREE BOOKS

TICKET 5
We're giving away brand new books to selected individuals. Scratch PINK METALLIC STRIP for number of free books you will receive.

AUTHORIZATION CODE

130107-742

FREE GIFT

TICKET 6
We have an outstanding added gift for you if you are accepting our free books. Scratch PINK METALLIC STRIP to reveal gift.

AUTHORIZATION CODE

130107-742

YES! Enter my Lucky Numbers in THE BIG WIN Sweepstakes and when winners are selected, tell me if I've won any prize. If the PINK METALLIC STRIP is scratched off on ticket #5, I will also receive one or more FREE Silhouette Desire® novels along with the FREE GIFT on ticket #6, as explained on the back and on the opposite page.

NAME _____   326 CIS AH9C (C-SIL-D-06/93)

ADDRESS _____ APT. _____

CITY _____ PROVINCE _____ POSTAL CODE _____

Book offer limited to one per household and not valid to current Silhouette Desire subscribers. All orders subject to approval

PRINTED IN U.S.A.   © 1991 HARLEQUIN ENTERPRISES LIMITED.

THE SILHOUETTE READER SERVICE™: HERE'S HOW IT WORKS

Accepting free books puts you under no obligation to buy anything. You may keep the books and gift and return the shipping statement marked ''cancel.'' If you do not cancel, about a month later we will send you 6 additional novels, and bill you just $2.49 each plus 25¢ delivery and GST*. That's the complete price, and—compared to cover prices of $2.99 each—quite a bargain! You may cancel at any time, but if you choose to continue, every month we'll send you 6 more books, which you may either purchase at the discount price . . . or return at our expense and cancel your subscription.

* Terms and prices subject to change without notice. Canadian residents will be charged applicable provincial taxes and GST.

Business Reply Mail

No Postage Stamp
Necessary if Mailed
in Canada

Postage will be paid by

SILHOUETTE READER SERVICE
PO BOX 609
FORT ERIE, ONT.
L2A 9Z9

Canada Post
Postes Canada
125

manipulated the slowdown purposely, of course. But Garth didn't know that.

"I—I can learn," she stuttered. "This is important to me, Garth. Please let me try."

Garth scrutinized the magnificent quarter horse stallion. "He's a good-looking animal. It would be a shame to put him down."

"It's settled, then," Candy said. "I'll work with him." She put her arms around Garth's waist and hugged him. "Thanks, Garth."

Garth folded Candy into his embrace. "Don't think it's going to be a picnic, because it isn't."

"Oh, I know that. But if Midnight can be tamed, you'll show me how to do it."

"I'm glad you have so much confidence in me." Garth was appalled by how good her compliment made him feel. It was one more sign of what he had begun to recognize as his growing dependence on her. He wasn't sure how it had happened, because nothing had changed in his life. At least not where outward appearances were concerned.

He still worked from dawn to dusk, only with Candy by his side. After supper in the dining room—he hadn't been stubborn fool enough to insist they keep on eating in the kitchen—he and Candy would retire to the parlor where she would read and he would work on the business end of his business. Then they would retire to his bedroom, where he would make love to her once or twice or sometimes even three times in a night.

She was always willing, and she had learned enough over the past week to incite him to passions even he hadn't known he was capable of. He felt his loins tighten as vivid memories of their lovemaking replayed in his head. The tastes, the scents, the sounds all combined to bring him to full arousal.

"Damn!"

Candy looked up at him. "What's wrong?" Then she looked down and said, "Oh. Again?"

"Again. Always. Constantly."

She grinned. "I think it's kind of cute."

He shook his head and laughed. "You would." His body concealed hers from the cowboys who were working nearby. He slipped his hand between them and cupped her breast, running his thumb across the nipple, which peaked instantly.

Candy made a tiny, kittenish sound in her throat and repaid him by sliding her hand across the hard ridge in his jeans. "Two can play that game," she teased.

They touched each other, hands pressing, pinching, playing, always careful to keep what they were doing hidden from the men who worked around them.

Only they might as well not have wasted their time. There wasn't a cowhand at Hawk's Way who

didn't know the boss had a soft spot for Candy
Baylor, and any look crosswise at her was a sure
way to find oneself booted off the ranch.

Candy was breathless by the time Garth called a
halt to their sensual play. He simply pulled her into
his arms and hugged her tight.

"We've got work to do, woman," he growled in
her ear. He turned her and gave her a little shove in
the direction of the stable.

As they fed the horses their evening ration of
grain and alfalfa hay, Candy asked, "Will you tell
me what I should do first, where I should start, to
tame the stud?"

"I'd leave him outside in the corral, give him
some room to move around. Don't hedge him in
too close."

Candy nodded her head. She could do that.

"You should be the one to feed and water him,
no one else. Talk to him when you do. Keep it soft,
something soothing."

"All right."

"Then you can start tempting him to come closer
with something sweet. Sugar works. Leave it where
he can find it at first. On the fence rail, maybe.
Then make him come to you for it."

"Won't he try to bite me?"

"He might. When the time comes, watch yourself."

"Then what?"

"When he starts coming to you for the sugar, you'll have a chance to touch him. Take your time. Move slow. Don't crowd him. Let him get to know you."

"And when he gets to know me, I can put a rope on him," Candy concluded.

"Hell, no, woman! You'd undo everything you've done so far."

Candy stepped out of a stall and stuck her hands on her hips. "How long before I can put a rope on him?" she demanded.

Garth shrugged. "It'll take time. Maybe a few weeks. A month. Six months. Maybe never."

"When will I know for sure?"

"You'll know when you know," Garth said. "There's no predicting these things. It all depends on the horse, on his history. If he can't let go of what happened in the past, of whatever it was that made him the way he is, he'll be useless to himself and everybody else."

"I see," Candy said thoughtfully. "Oh, I see."

Candy looked at Garth with new eyes. She couldn't help seeing the similarity between the battle she was fighting in her attempts to gain Garth's love and trust and the challenge of taming the wild stallion.

She was determined to win the stallion's confidence. She would do whatever was necessary to save the animal from destruction. And if she could win one battle, surely she could win the other.

"All right, Garth. I'll do what you say."

"You just be careful," Garth said. "That beast is dangerous. He'll destroy you if he can."

Candy was struck by Garth's warning. So, too, could *he* destroy *her,* if he only knew it. But she was her father's daughter, and she wasn't used to giving up or giving in. She would tame the stallion *and* the man. Just wait and see if she didn't!

Garth put his arm around Candy as they walked back toward the house. "By the way," he said, "we'll be having company for the Labor Day holiday."

"Oh?"

"My sister Tate's son is being christened. The whole family will be coming here for the occasion."

Garth felt Candy hesitate, then slow to a stop. She turned to face him and asked, "Where do I fit into that picture, Garth?"

"You'll be staying with me, of course. Just like you have been for the past week."

Candy shook her head. "I don't think so."

"Why not?" Garth wasn't happy about the irritation in his voice. It indicated just how great was his need to have her in his bed.

"I don't want your family thinking—"

"Don't worry. They won't say a word." He would give them fair warning that Candy was different. He couldn't—wouldn't—tolerate his brothers saying the things about Candy that they had said about other women he had from time to time brought to Hawk's Way.

"But they'll know," Candy protested.

"Know what?"

That I'm sleeping with you when you haven't once said you love me, Candy thought. She didn't dare say that aloud.

"How soon did you say they'll be here?" she asked.

"Labor Day."

Only three weeks in which to get Garth to admit his feelings for her.

Candy didn't waste any time following Garth's advice, either with the horse or with him. She kept one rule in mind at all times.

Give him some room to move around. Don't hedge him in too close. With that understood she moved on to the second point Garth had made.

You should be the one to feed and water him, no one else. She was the only one who fed and watered the stallion. Things were a little more difficult when it came to feeding Garth.

Charlie One Horse normally prepared meals. Candy decided to take the bull by the horns and tell

Charlie what she was trying to do. She caught him in the kitchen preparing supper.

When she was done, the old Indian tugged on the beaded rawhide thong that held one of his braids and asked, "You really think this is goin' to work?"

"It has to," Candy said.

Charlie was skeptical that Garth would ever trust another woman after what his momma had done. Mona's infidelity had occurred at a very impressionable time in Garth's life. But he had seen with his own eyes that Garth treated Candy differently than he had other women. And Charlie had been the one to wash the bloodstained sheets that had told their own story.

"All right," Charlie said at last. "I ain't gone on vacation yet this year. I'll tell Garth I'm takin' three weeks off. But that's all. I ain't missin' the christenin'."

"I'd never ask you to do that," Candy said. She gave the old man a kiss on the cheek and watched his ruddy face turn even ruddier. "Thank you, Charlie."

"Aw. Didn't do nothin'."

"How soon can you leave?" Candy asked.

Charlie chuckled. "I'll be gone 'fore supper, if that's what you're askin'."

"Thanks again, Charlie."

"Good luck, girl," Charlie said. As she left Charlie to run upstairs and change her clothes he muttered, "You're gonna need it!"

While she cooked supper, Candy went over in her mind the rest of what Garth had said about taming the stallion. *Talk to him. Keep it soft, something soothing.*

Garth wasn't in the best of moods that evening. As Candy set his plate in front of him he grumbled, "That old buzzard didn't even give me a day of warning. Who's going to do the cooking around here?"

"I am."

Garth eyed her skeptically. "You can cook?"

"Of course I can."

"You've already got enough to do. How are you going to handle any more?"

"I'll manage," Candy said. "Don't worry about me, darling." Candy let the endearment drop in a husky, breathless voice.

Garth looked at her sharply, but he didn't deny her the right to call him by such a term. Candy joined him at the table and waited for the conversation to start. She soon discovered how much Charlie had contributed to the dinnertime talk. Charlie usually asked one or the other of them how the day had gone, and then they would answer him. Candy had never noticed before that she and Garth had been talking to Charlie, not to each other.

Their time in the parlor after supper each evening had always been comfortable because they were together, even though very little dialogue passed between them. Candy recognized the importance of Garth's lesson. She needed to talk to him, to establish some sort of communication with him beyond the exchange of knowledge that consumed their days and the lovemaking that consumed their nights.

"Tell me what it was like growing up at Hawk's Way," she said.

Garth seemed startled by the request. She was afraid for a moment he wouldn't respond. Then he said, "There was a lot of work to do. I did it."

"There must have been some time for play," Candy chided.

"Not much," Garth muttered.

"But there were so many of you—your father and your brothers and sister—to do the work, and with the cowhands—"

"We couldn't afford hired help when I was growing up," Garth interrupted.

"Oh. Hawk's Way is so large and successful now, I thought it must always have been like this."

"It's always been a big spread," Garth conceded, "but we've been through a lot of hard times. There's oil on the property, but the bottom fell out of the market, if you'll recall. We raised beef for a while, but that's another market that isn't too dependable. Then we took a chance on raising rodeo stock. It wasn't until we started breeding and training championship cutting horses that we could afford any outside help.''

''I had no idea,'' Candy said. It gave her a whole different image of what Garth's childhood must have been like.

''I saw a picture of your father upstairs. You must miss him a lot.''

An agonized look crossed Garth's face and was gone so quickly Candy thought she must have imagined it.

''He was a good father. Until my mother killed him.''

''What?! Faron told me three years ago that your father came off a bronc and broke his neck. Are you saying he lied?''

Candy waited for Garth to answer her question, to explain his provocative statement, but his features turned stony and he remained mute. At least she knew now why there was no picture of his mother upstairs. Finally, she couldn't stand the suspense any longer.

''I don't want to intrude on what must be a painful episode in your life—''

''Then don't,'' he said in a harsh voice.

Candy reminded herself this was supposed to be *soothing* talk and decided to change the subject.

''Tell me more about your brothers and sister.''

Almost immediately his expression softened. "My brother Jesse's a renegade," Garth said. "We were too close in age, so we knocked heads after Dad died. Jesse left to find his own way."

"How long was he gone?"

"It was years before we heard from him again. He was a Texas Ranger until he married a widow named Honey Farrell. Now he has two stepsons and a daughter of his own, and he and Honey run their ranch, the Flying Diamond, in southwest Texas.

"My sister Tate is as independent as they come. Did you know she ran away from home?"

"You must have been crazy with worry," Candy said.

"I was. But at twenty-three she decided she'd had enough of her overprotective older brothers."

"Twenty-three!" Candy gasped. "You're kidding, right?"

"I'm afraid not," Garth said with a rueful laugh. "She was gone for a couple of months before my long-lost brother Jesse called out of the blue and told us Tate had moved in with some rancher in south Texas. My brothers and I showed up the next day and made things legal."

Candy was aghast. "You forced her to get married?"

"She was pregnant," Garth said flatly. "But it wouldn't have mattered whether she was or not. She was an innocent when she met Adam Philips. He shouldn't have taken advantage of her. Anyway, everything turned out all right. Tate and Adam are bringing their son, Brett, here to be christened.''

Candy bit her tongue to keep from making the retort that leapt to mind. But if Garth wasn't making the connection between Adam's treatment of Garth's sister and Garth's treatment of her, she would be wasting her breath to point it out to him.

"What about the brother I met three years ago, Faron?"

"You mean my brother the lover?" Garth said with a chuckle.

Candy laughed as she recalled the way Faron had flirted with her. "That's the one. You said he was away on business. What kind?"

A hard, closed look reappeared on Garth's face. "Faron's in Wyoming meeting his stepmother."

Candy's brow furrowed in confusion. "What? How can Faron have a stepmother if he's your brother?"

"You figure it out." Garth's tone of voice made it clear he was done with that line of discussion. He was also finished with supper. He picked up his plate and carried it out to the kitchen, leaving Candy sitting alone.

She wouldn't have called her efforts a total success, but she had learned more personal information about Garth over supper this evening than in all the time she had spent at Hawk's Way. That achievement gave her the confidence to go on to the next step in Garth's training program.

You can start tempting him to come closer with something sweet. Sugar works. Leave it where he can find it at first. On the fence rail, maybe. Then make him come to you for it.

Candy picked up her plate and headed for the kitchen after Garth. He had already rinsed his plate and stacked it in the dishwasher and was making himself a cup of coffee.

"I'll have one of those," Candy said as she rinsed her own plate.

Garth took out another mug and poured her a cup. He handed it to her, and she took a sip before setting it down on the counter. She walked up to Garth, put her hands around his waist and leaned her cheek against his chest.

"Mmm. This feels good."

Garth said nothing. Candy's hands slid down over the contours of his buttocks and back up the center of his spine to his nape, where she played with the hair that hung over his collar. She turned her face slightly and nipped his flesh through his shirt.

"Sonofabitch," Garth muttered.

Candy released him and walked away as though she hadn't felt the blunt ridge in his jeans. She used her hands to lever herself into a sitting position on the heavy oak table. Then she spread her knees and leaned back on her palms.

Come and get your sugar, darling.

Garth approached her slowly until he stood between her legs. He grasped her thighs and pulled her toward him until the heart of her was pressed to the heat of him. Then he pressed her shoulders down until she was lying flat on the table.

When he comes to you for the sugar, you'll have a chance to touch him. Take your time. Move slow. Don't crowd him. Let him get to know you.

Candy didn't move a hair when Garth reached for the snap of her jeans. Nor did she take her eyes off him as the zipper rasped down. He placed his hand flat on her belly and slid his thumb down so it just grazed her mound. She gasped. But she let him have his way.

He stepped back and pulled off her boots and socks. Then he reached his hands into the back of her jeans and began pulling them down. She lifted her hips slightly to help him. She lay before him naked from the waist down.

His dark eyes were almost black, hooded with desire. A muscle jerked in his cheek. He was breathing hard, as though he had been running. She wasn't breathing so well herself.

He pulled her to the edge of the table again and spread her legs so that she was totally exposed to him. Candy resisted the urge to cover herself. Instead she reached out and covered his hands where they lay on her naked thighs. She trailed her hands up his arms.

She knew what was coming. He left her plenty of time to refuse as he lifted her up and lowered his mouth to kiss her nether lips. Her hands tightened on his arms as a thrill of pleasure raced through her. Her eyes never left his face as he made love to her in this new and very different way. The sensations were exquisite, unbearably exciting, unbelievably arousing. He possessed her totally, absolutely, bringing her to a climax so powerful she trembled afterward.

She wanted to tell Garth what she was feeling. How wonderful the gift was that he had given her. But she couldn't catch her breath, and wouldn't have known what words to use anyway. She lay before him, her heart in her eyes, telling him in the only way she could that she loved him. That she wanted to spend her life with him.

How long before I can put a rope on him?

It'll take time. Maybe a few weeks. A month. Six months. Maybe never.

She managed to sit up. He was still standing between her legs. She reached out for the snap of his jeans but his hand was there to stop her. She waited to see what he would do. What he would say.

He only muttered, "Sonofabitch." Then he picked her up in his arms and headed upstairs. "Come on, woman. Let's go to bed."

Garth loved Candy with his whole body, in every way he knew and some he made up on the spot. He had nearly gone crazy when she had loved him the same way he had loved her in the kitchen. It had been wonderful. Beyond anything he had ever imagined it could be. He could feel her waiting for the words of love. He could almost hear them ricocheting off the walls. But he didn't speak them.

Neither did she.

Candy lay in Garth's arms, replete. But not satisfied.

When will I know for sure?

You'll know when you know. There's no predicting these things.

Candy had to figure out what it was that had made Garth so reluctant to commit himself to a woman. He had given her several clues. First, there was the fact that he had no picture of his mother anywhere in the house. Second, he had said that his mother killed his father. Finally, there was that story of Faron having a stepmother, because he had a different father.

It came to her in a flash, so obvious that she wondered why she hadn't suspected it before.

Apparently, Garth's mother had been unfaithful to his father. Faron had been the result. And

Garth had never trusted another woman to be any more faithful than his mother.

At least now she knew what she was up against.

If he can't let go of the past, whatever it was that made him the way he is, he'll be useless to himself and everybody else.

Candy felt overwhelmed by her sudden knowledge. How was she going to change Garth's lifetime of distrust? What could she possibly do to convince him that she would never be unfaithful to him? It just wasn't possible.

She remembered the last of Garth's warnings when he had told her how to tame the big stud.

You be careful. That beast is dangerous. He'll destroy you if he can.

Candy turned into Garth's arms. She felt them close tight around her. At least for now he was hers, and she was his. She would hold him with the only ropes she had. Somehow, someday, she would find a way to reach him. She was sure of it. She would start tomorrow with that black beast in the corral and prove it could be done.

Seven

Candy had won several battles with the savage black stallion, but she was losing the war. No matter how hard she tried, the animal refused to trust her. Her failure left her feeling desolate because she had tied all her hopes for a life with Garth to her success with the incorrigible stallion. They were both turning out to be unbelievably stubborn males.

She had gotten only so far with Garth and no farther. She couldn't explain it exactly, but it seemed like the more they made love, the more distant he became. Not that he desired her any less. In fact, their loving sometimes seemed almost desperately passionate, as though they had only these moments, these very few moments, to love each other.

And maybe this summer would be all they ever had together.

Candy held out the sugar to the black again. "Come here, you big beastie. Come here and take what I'm offering you. Everything is going to be all right. No one's ever going to hurt you again."

The black horse stomped a hoof and shook his head.

"You don't believe me, do you?" She slumped against the corral. "Neither does he. He doesn't trust me any more now than he did the day I came here. He wants me. But he doesn't trust me."

Garth's family was due to start arriving any day and Candy hadn't yet made up her mind what she was going to do. She couldn't bear to have Garth's family think she was just another one of the women moving through his life. Yet he had given her no encouragement to think that she would ever play a continuing role in his future.

She stepped onto the bottom rail of the corral and leaned over, holding out her hand with the cube of sugar in it. The stallion neighed and stood his ground.

"Come here, you bullheaded mule," she crooned to him.

The horse took two steps forward and stopped.

"That's it, you willful devil," she purred. "Come and get it."

Suddenly she felt Garth's dark, brooding gaze on her. She turned to face him and lost her balance. He caught her as she fell.

The stallion raced back to the other side of the corral.

"Dammit, Garth! I almost had him," she exploded. She tried to wrench herself from his grasp, but he refused to let her go.

"Whoa, there, girl! I came to tell you Jesse and Honey are here with their kids. I thought you might like to come and meet them."

Candy took one look down at the ragged jeans and dirty shirt she had been working in all day and groaned. "Look at me. I'm a mess."

"I wouldn't say that." Garth tightened his arms around her. "You look fine to me," he whispered.

She shivered at the feel of his warm breath against her face. "You'd think I looked fine no matter what I was wearing—or wasn't wearing. I wish you'd reminded me they were coming today, Garth. I wanted to make a good impression on your family."

"Why bother? They'll be leaving in a few days anyway." He brushed her long blond hair out of the way and kissed her nape.

Candy hid her face against Garth's chest. How dense could a man be? If she married him she would certainly be seeing his family more than just this once! But that was the problem. Garth apparently didn't see a future that included her.

"Hello there."

Candy jerked herself from Garth's embrace at the sound of a deep male voice. Her face flushed scarlet as she turned to face a man she realized must be Garth's brother. She crossed her arms protectively around herself. "H-hello."

"I'm Jesse. You must be Candy Baylor. Garth was telling us about you."

Candy shot a glance at Garth. Exactly what had he been saying? She took the hand Jesse offered and shook it. "It's nice to meet you, Jesse."

She compared Jesse to his brother and noted Jesse's skin was a darker bronze, his features broader, blunter. He had the same thick black hair as Garth, the same dark eyes—only Jesse's seemed more remote.

Garth reached out to put a hand back around her shoulder, but she stepped out of his way.

"I have to go change," she said. "It's getting on toward time for supper."

She hurried past them and headed for the kitchen door.

Candy took one step inside the house and froze. It looked like an army had invaded. There was a collection of baby furniture stuck in corners and baby paraphernalia littered the counters and table.

She should have realized the kitchen was the very place where everyone would congregate. To her dismay not only did she find Honey there, but Tate and her husband, Adam, as well.

She recognized Jesse's wife, Honey, right away because Garth had said she had long, curly blond hair and striking blue eyes. Tate was a delicate version of her brothers, with short-cropped black hair and friendly hazel eyes. Blond-haired, blue-eyed Adam was clearly no Whitelaw.

Candy opened her mouth and shut it again, unsure where to start.

Charlie stepped into the breach. "All you folks, this here is Candy Baylor. She's workin' at Hawk's Way this summer, learnin' all about cuttin' horses. Candy, these folks are Jesse and his wife, Honey, and Tate and her husband, Adam. Them babies in the cribs is Lauren and Brett. Honey and Jesse's two boys, Jack and Jonathan, are upstairs. You'll meet them later."

Candy shook hands with the men, and despite the condition of her work clothes, got a hug from each of the women. She resisted the urge to go look at the babies. "It's nice to meet you all," she said. "I hope you'll excuse me. I need to clean up a little."

"Sure," Tate said. "Hurry back down. I want to hear what my big brother has been doing all summer."

"Giving orders," Candy muttered.

"What was that?" Tate asked.

Honey rescued Candy from having to reply by putting a hand on her shoulder and heading her in the direction of the door. "Go on and change. We'll still be here when you get back."

Candy took her time in the shower. By the time she got back downstairs, dressed in a clean pair of jeans and a Western shirt—the same thing the two women in the kitchen had been wearing—everyone had resettled in the parlor. Apparently the two boys were still playing upstairs.

Honey was sitting in Jesse's lap on a chair in front of the fireplace. Adam and Tate were sitting close beside each other on the couch. Garth was standing with an arm resting on the thick pine mantel above the stone fireplace. They were discussing—arguing—the merits of two brands of horse feed.

It wasn't the adults who interested her. Like a lodestone, Candy approached the antique cradles in the corner that held the two babies. She tucked Brett's blanket around him, then tentatively reached down to caress the black curls on Lauren's head.

"Go ahead and pick her up," Honey said. "She won't bite."

"Are you sure you don't mind?" Candy asked.

Honey didn't answer, just got up and crossed to the cradle. She picked up her daughter and laid her in Candy's arms. "Be sure to support her head."

"What if I drop her?"

"You won't," Honey said as she settled herself back in Jesse's lap.

Candy had always loved babies. Maybe it was because she had never had any brothers or sisters of her own. Unfortunately, she had come into very little contact with small children during her twenty years. She was fascinated by Lauren's tiny fingers and her equally tiny fingernails. She laughed when the baby grasped her hand.

"She's so strong!"

Candy looked up and found herself staring straight into Garth's dark eyes. She didn't know when he had crossed from the hearth. She hadn't heard him coming. But then, she had been totally involved with investigating the baby.

Garth felt his stomach fall all the way to his toes at the sight of Candy with a child in her arms. She looked so...maternal. He had never planned to have a wife, and he would never bring a child into the world without the benefit of marriage. He had long ago resigned himself to the fact that he would never have children. He had settled for the idea of standing on the sidelines, of being a fond uncle.

Now he could see how he had cheated himself all these years. Of the joy of having his own child. Of the opportunity of sharing that bliss with a woman he loved. It hurt. Lord, it hurt.

His jaw tightened. He might never feel the joy of having his own child, but he would likewise never be destroyed by the pain of a woman's betrayal. He could survive the former, but not the latter.

"Do you want to hold her?" Candy asked.

The hell of it was, he did. "Sure," he said.

Candy laid the baby in his arms. To her surprise Garth seemed perfectly comfortable. "You look like you've done this before."

He shot a glance over his shoulder at Tate. "I put a diaper or two on my sister over the years."

Tate blushed. "Good grief, Garth. Do you have to remind me of that?"

"I somehow can't imagine you diapering a baby," Candy said to Garth with a grin.

"Mom died when Tate was born," he said in a harsh voice. "Dad fell apart and Charlie was busy with Jesse and Faron. That left me."

There was a long silence.

"I didn't know," Candy said. "That must have been hard on you."

Garth laid the baby back in the crib and returned to his place by the mantel. "She kept me up a few nights. But it was worth it."

Candy saw the look Garth exchanged with Tate. There was love there, and concern. Love for family wasn't the same as romantic love, but she couldn't help feeling optimistic. Surely there must be a way to convince Garth that loving a woman didn't have to end in disaster.

The sound of footsteps in the foyer alerted them to the fact that someone else had arrived.

"That'll be Faron," Garth said. "We're in the parlor, Faron," he called to his brother.

Candy took her time looking at the third Whitelaw brother. She had met Faron before but saw him differently now that she knew he had a different father than the other Whitelaw men. His eyes were an unusual gray-green color. He had black hair, like the rest of the Whitelaws, but his facial features were more refined. He was unbelievably handsome.

Faron wasn't alone. He had two women with him, an arm around each of them. "This is my grandmother, Madelyn Prescott," he said. "I call her Maddy."

The younger woman with Faron, an elegantly tall blonde with stunning violet eyes, was clearly uncomfortable. The woman seemed on the verge of fleeing the room. Faron introduced her as his stepmother, Belinda Prescott.

"That's the ugly stepmother?" Jesse whispered. His wife elbowed him in the ribs to shut him up. That saved Candy the trouble of kicking him.

Obviously the whole family knew of Faron's illegitimate birth. But it was clear there was something else going on between him and his beautiful young stepmother.

Garth spoke first in what had become a very awkward situation. "I'm pleased to meet you, Belinda."

Candy knew Garth well enough by now to hear the sneer in his voice. It was plain what he thought of the beautiful young woman who had married a rich man old enough to be her father. *Not much.*

Candy couldn't stand it. She reached out and grasped Belinda's hand.

"Hi. I'm Candice—Candy Baylor. I guess you and I are the only two people here who aren't family." She smiled, giving Belinda the welcome Garth hadn't.

"I'm working at Hawk's Way this summer, and I can imagine how you must feel, meeting this rowdy bunch for the first time."

"They are a little overwhelming," Belinda said.

Candy watched as Faron stepped up and put his arm around Belinda to support her. He reached out his hand to Candy and said, "I don't know if you remember me."

"Of course I remember you," Candy said. "Last time I was here with my father you yanked my braids at the breakfast table."

Faron grinned. "Guilty. Was that only three years ago? You've grown a little since then."

The longer Garth watched his brother flirting with Candy, the more irritated he got. Faron was a man who loved women. And they loved him. Garth wasn't about to let Faron work his wiles on Candy. "I think it's time you showed Maddy and Belinda where they'll be staying," he said.

The moment the three latest arrivals headed upstairs, Garth turned to Candy and said, "You come with me. There's a mare due to foal in the next day or so that needs to be checked."

Candy was furious that Garth had ordered her to come with him like some hired hand rather than asking her if she wanted to go. Besides, this was the first she had heard about a foaling mare. She wasn't sure Garth hadn't made the whole thing up to get her out of the room. Candy would have argued if Garth's brother and sister and their spouses hadn't been sitting there with ears perked up listening.

"All right," she said. Once they were out of earshot she planned to give Garth a good piece of her mind. But Garth was striding so fast it was all she could do to keep up with him.

The instant they reached the barn, Garth turned on her. "What the hell did you think you were doing in there?"

Candy was completely taken aback by his attack. "What are you talking about?"

"I'm talking about the way you were flirting with Faron."

"Flirting with—"

"He's right, though, you have grown up a lot in three years. I've noticed the difference myself. You're not a kid anymore, are you?"

He grabbed her wrists and pinned them over her head, then backed her up against the rough wooden wall, grinding his hips against hers. To Candy's surprise, he was aroused. To her utter horror, his violent actions caused a rush of desire to flood her body.

He put both of her wrists in one hand, then reached down to free the snap on her jeans. He unzipped them and yanked them down past her buttocks, then freed himself.

"Garth, I don't—"

"You belong to me. No one else. You're *mine!*"

He punctuated the word by thrusting inside her. Candy's body undulated to accommodate his intrusion. His mouth found hers and his tongue forced its way inside. There was nothing gentle about his lovemaking. It was hard and fast and desperate as it had never been before.

It was rough, but it wasn't rape. Because Candy participated wholeheartedly in everything he did. She sucked his tongue into her mouth and parried with her own. She arched her body into his, forcing him to give and give until at last he cried out in exultation. Her own body shuddered in response.

He released her hands at last and pulled her tight against him. He hid his face at her throat. They were both panting with exhaustion, and if either had tried to move they both would have fallen. At last he let her go.

Candy felt bereft when he turned his back on her. She heard his zipper and realized that only the tails of her shirt kept her decent. She turned away to tuck in her shirt and rearrange her jeans. What must he think of her? She had been totally wanton!

Garth shoved all ten fingers through his hair. He had never lost control like that with a woman. Never! He dared a glance at Candy and saw that her lips were swollen, her face flushed. He felt his body responding at the sight and swore loud and long.

Candy's face suddenly bleached white. She knew Garth was wishing she had never come here. She knew he was going to send her away right now, today. And she knew she would go rather than face his family when he felt about her the way he obviously did. "I guess you want me out of here," she said.

"There's a mare that needs looking after," he said. "Unless you're ready to quit and go home."

Candy could hardly believe her ears. There actually *was* a foaling mare! And he wasn't sending her away. "I'm not a quitter," she said. There were things that needed to be said about his irrational fear of Faron's charm, about the way he had made violent love to her. But she knew now there would be time enough later to say them. "Let's go see about that mare."

The pregnant mare had been separated from the other animals at the far end of the barn. In the later stages of the birth she would lie down, but right now she was restlessly pacing the stall.

"Is this the first time she's foaled?" Candy asked.

Garth shook his head. "Second. She had some difficulty the first time, but got through it all right. I have the vet on call in case she has trouble again, but I'm not expecting it."

Garth stepped into the stall and talked soothingly to the mare. "Easy there, Starlight. You're going to be fine. Take it easy, girl." As he ran his hands over the mare's sides he called to Candy. "Come in here a minute."

Candy walked quietly—if not calmly—up beside him.

"Put your hand here."

She did as he asked.

"What do you feel?"

Candy's brows rose in surprise. "Contractions."

Garth nodded. "Right. I don't like the fact she's so restless. I think I'll stay with her tonight. The company might calm her down."

"What about your family?" Candy asked.

"They're all ranchers themselves. They'll understand my stock comes first."

"If you're staying, I'm staying," Candy said. She would much rather spend the time with Garth than endure the speculative looks of his brothers and sister and their spouses.

"Suit yourself," Garth said. "If you ask Charlie, he'll fix us some sandwiches and a thermos of coffee to tide us over tonight. I'll get some blankets from the tack room."

Candy took her time getting back to the kitchen. At the last minute she checked to make sure no sign remained of her lovemaking with Garth in the barn. To her chagrin, her shirt was hanging half in and half out of her jeans. She stopped and tucked it in neatly, then shoved her hands through her hair in hopes of straightening a few of the tangles.

Candy stood at the screen door and watched the antics inside with amazement. Everybody seemed to be in the kitchen helping with supper. Perhaps *helping* was the wrong word. They seemed to be *playing* catch with a raw potato. Tate threw it to— or was she throwing it at?—Faron, who caught it and tossed it to Jesse, who tossed it to Honey, who tossed it to Adam, who tossed it back to Tate. Tate then handed it to Charlie One Horse, who cut it into four pieces and dropped it into a pot of water on the stove.

Candy took advantage of the laughter that followed to quickly step inside.

"Where's Garth?" Faron asked.

"He's in the barn," she answered. "He sent me in to let you know we're going to be spending the night there."

Faron cocked a brow. "Oh, really?"

Candy flushed as she realized Faron had misinterpreted her words. "There's a mare foaling," she rushed to explain. "Garth thinks it would calm her down to have company. So we're going to stay with her."

Faron looked at Tate, who looked at Jesse, who looked back at Faron. Garth had brought a lot of women to Hawk's Way, but he had always kept ranch business and his personal pleasure separate in the past. To be honest, none of the women Garth had ever invited to the ranch would have been willing to spend the night sleeping on a blanket in the hay, let alone baby-sitting a nervous mare.

So the three of them took a second look at Candy Baylor.

Candy tried to ignore the measuring eyes she felt on her as she crossed to Charlie One Horse. "Garth said you'd fix us up a thermos of coffee. I'll make us some sandwiches, since we won't be here for supper.''

She was on her way back out the door when Tate stopped her.

"You don't have to spend the night in the barn if you'd rather not," Tate said. "My eldest brother can be something of a bully."

Candy appreciated Tate's concern, but she hurried to reassure the young woman that she wasn't acting under duress. "I came here to learn everything I can about managing a place like Hawk's Way. I'm looking forward to watching this birth. I've never seen a foal born before."

"Never?" Tate asked. "It can be a pretty messy proposition. Are you sure you want to be there?"

Candy nodded her head. "Garth will be there."

Candy didn't realize until the words were out what she had revealed to Tate. Her absolute confidence in Garth. Her absolute certainty that if he was by her side, there was nothing she couldn't handle.

Tate smiled. "Well, well."

There was nothing more Candy could say without making the situation worse than it already was. "I'd better get going. Garth will be waiting for me."

She flushed when she realized how that sounded.

"I mean," she corrected, "he'll be getting hungry."

That was even worse.

"For *supper*," she stressed.

Tate burst out laughing. She nudged Candy out the kitchen door. "Don't worry about us, we'll all be fine. I just hope that mare delivers in time for you two to come to the christening tomorrow."

"Oh, Garth would never—"

Tate shook her head. "I'm afraid you don't know my brother as well as you think. The ranch comes first—always. You won't find anyone here who doesn't understand that. I think all of us love Hawk's Way, but to Garth... It's all Garth will ever have."

Candy heard the caution in Tate's voice. Garth's sister was telling her that while the rest of the Whitelaws might marry and have families, Garth would not. Candy was being warned not to offer Garth her heart, because he would most likely break it.

Candy understood. But she didn't agree. At least, she didn't want to agree. She had seen signs that Garth might let her climb over, step across or otherwise breach the wall he had built over the years to keep himself safe from hurt. She refused to be discouraged by Tate's well-intentioned warning.

"I'll be careful," Candy said.

Before Tate could say anything more, Candy clutched the thermos and the bag of sandwiches close and hurried out the screen door.

The contrast between the sunlight outside and the dimness of the barn left Candy blind for the few seconds it took her eyes to adjust. She called out to Garth, but got no answer.

"Garth?" she repeated. Still no answer. She felt a sudden anxiety. Something was wrong.

She rushed a few steps farther into the barn, even though she was still having trouble seeing. Which was when she tripped over the wheelbarrow.

Garth saw the sandwiches and thermos go flying in one direction while Candy went the other. He got to her just before she hit the ground. She clutched at him, and it was all he could do to keep from falling with her.

With effort he regained his balance and stood her on her feet. She was still trembling, so he kept his arms around her. His own heart was beating fast from his terror at seeing her about to crack her head on the cement floor. He tightened his grasp, aware of what a narrow escape she'd had.

"Lord almighty, woman! How did you miss seeing that wheelbarrow?" he said angrily.

"Where were you, Garth? I called and you didn't answer," she retorted no less angrily.

"I was trying to make someplace comfortable for you to spend the night," he snapped back.

They glared at each other for another moment before Candy lowered her eyes and hid her face against Garth's chest.

"I thought something had happened to you," she murmured. "I guess I panicked."

"I guess you did," Garth said in a husky voice. He felt a heaviness in his groin, a growing tension that arose from holding her in his arms. He wanted her again.

His need for her frightened him more than he was willing to admit. Once again he pushed her away. To protect himself. And ultimately, to protect her.

Garth let Candy's feet drop and held on just long enough to make sure she was steady on them before he said, "I didn't hear the thermos hit, so maybe it landed in some hay. See if you can find it without falling down again."

Candy was stung by Garth's insinuation that she was clumsy. She marched over to the stall where the thermos had indeed landed safely on a pile of hay and picked it up.

"Here it is," she said. "Catch."

That was all the warning Garth got before she threw it to him. He had already picked up the bag of sandwiches and was forced to drop it again in order to catch the thermos.

Candy walked over, picked up the bag of sandwiches and held them out to Garth. "You dropped something," she said in a sweet voice.

Garth opened his mouth and shut it again.

Candy laughed at the look of chagrin on his face.

Garth turned his back on Candy and headed toward the stall next to the one where the mare was treading. "Come on. Let's eat."

Candy thought twice about following him. She didn't understand how Garth could be so gentle one moment and so harsh the next. And lately he had no sense of humor. But she was hungry, and going back to the house for more sandwiches would require an explanation she would rather not make.

She found Garth sitting on a thick pile of hay he had covered with a wool blanket. He was leaning back against the side of the stall. He had a cup of coffee in one hand and a roast beef sandwich in the other. Candy joined him, but kept to the farthest edge of the blanket. She helped herself to a cup of coffee from the thermos and grabbed one of the sandwiches.

They ate without conversing. Candy focused her attention on the mare.

"Starlight seems a little quieter," she said.

"Her labor's stopped."

"Is that normal?"

"It happens sometimes."

"Shouldn't we call the vet?" Candy asked anxiously.

"Not yet. We'll wait a while and see if it starts again."

But "a while" turned into several hours. Garth maintained a stony silence that discouraged conversation. Candy wasn't about to let him sulk all evening.

"Mrs. Prescott is very beautiful, don't you think?"

"Faron's stepmother? She's pretty enough."

"And very young."

Garth grunted an assent. "Not what Faron was expecting, that's for sure."

"Then it's true?"

"What's true?"

"Faron had a different father than the rest of you?"

The skin stretched tight across Garth's face. His fists bunched at his sides. "I try not to air the family linen in public."

"It must have been awful for you," she said.

"I survived," he said in a harsh voice. "I told you I don't want to talk about this."

"Why not?"

"You're asking me why I don't want to discuss the fact my mother was a whore!"

Candy scrambled to her feet. "How can you say such a thing about your own mother?"

Garth rose to his feet and towered over her. "Because it's true!"

"People make mistakes—"

"That ruin lives," Garth said ruthlessly. "My mother killed my father as surely as if she'd put a knife in him."

''He was bucked off a horse. He broke his neck. Your mother had nothing to do with that!''

''He was drunk! He was drunk a lot after he found out what she'd done.''

''But he forgave her!'' Candy protested.

''How the hell do you know that?''

She fisted her hands on her hips. ''Tate is proof of it!''

''Tate is no proof at all,'' Garth countered.

''Why not?'' Candy demanded. ''Your father had to make love to your mother to get her pregnant again.''

''He didn't make love to her,'' Garth said in an anguished voice. ''He raped her.''

Candy's face bleached white. ''Oh, no. Oh, my God, no!''

''Are you happy now?'' Garth put the heels of his hands to his eyes. ''I've never told that to another living soul.''

A moment later Candy's arms were around him. There was nothing she could say, so she said nothing.

Garth refused her comfort by physically removing her hands and stepping away from her. But now that the dam had been breached, he was unable to stop the flood of words that followed.

''Jesse and I were supposed to be spending the night with friends. I'd forgotten my jackknife, so I came back. Mom and Dad were arguing. She was begging him to forgive her, to let her make amends.

He told her he would never forgive her. He could never forget, either, because Faron was there to remind him every day of what she'd done. But he still intended to exercise his marital rights.

"She told him to stay away from her. That she couldn't bear for him to touch her anymore if all he wanted was sex.

"But he wouldn't be denied. He was stronger than she was. I...I couldn't leave without being discovered. So I heard it all. Her screams. His shouts. And her tears.

"He was sorry afterward. He begged her to forgive him. You see, his betrayal of their love was every bit as wrong—as horrible—as hers had been.

"There were complications, and my mother died in childbirth when Tate was born. And my father...my father cried. He was sorry she was dead. He didn't want to live without her. I think he found a way to kill himself."

Garth's voice had become progressively more guttural, his tone of voice more bitter, more cynical, until finally it ended in a harsh rasp.

Candy had listened in shock and horror to the ghastly circumstances that had molded Garth into the man he was. She felt an awful sense of despair. After hearing such a story, how could she hope to convince Garth that he could trust her? More frightening, how could she trust him not to turn on her as his father had turned on his mother?

"Garth, I—"

"Get out of here."

"I only want to offer you—"

"Sex? Sure, I'll be glad of it. It'll help me forget. That's what you want, isn't it? To make me forget my mother betrayed my father, and that he loved her so much he got himself killed rather than live without her!"

Garth took one step and grasped a handful of her silky blond hair. He yanked her head back so she was forced to look up at him. His arm snaked around her and pulled her tight against his hips.

Candy struggled with all her might. There was no way to deceive herself that this was love. It was something violent, something painful. And it would kill forever any feelings she had for him if she let him go through with it. She was certain Garth knew exactly how she felt, certain that he was driving her away to save her because he feared, as he had all these years, that if he ever loved a woman he might turn out to be just like his father.

"Garth, stop!" she said. "You aren't like him. You aren't! And I'm not like her. Don't make it impossible—"

"It *is* impossible! Don't you see that?"

"No!" she said fiercely. She fought back the tears that brimmed in her eyes.

"Don't fool yourself!" he said with a sneer.

"You're the fool, Garth Whitelaw. And I'm not going to stay here and let you do something you'll be sorry for later.'' She stomped hard on his instep. He yelped and let her go.

Candy raced from the barn, not looking back to see whether he was chasing her. She didn't stop until she reached the kitchen door. She paused then, to make sure there was no one inside to see the tears that fell in hot tracks on her cheeks.

She snuck in past the parlor where she saw the two mothers nursing their babies. It struck fresh pain in her heart to see her secret dreams played out in front of her and know she would never be a mother sitting there in front of the fireplace at Hawk's Way with Garth's baby at her breast.

She tiptoed up the stairs and closed her bedroom door behind her. She stared at the bed, knowing she would never be able to sleep.

Candy had to think what to do next. Maybe the time had come to leave Hawk's Way. She wouldn't be able to stand seeing Garth in pain and knowing he refused to reach out for the comfort—not necessarily sexual—she was willing to offer.

But maybe she ought to stay. And give him comfort whether he wanted it or not.

It was a long night. She was grateful for the sunrise, but she still hadn't made up her mind what to do. She would at least stay at Hawk's Way long enough to attend the christening. After that…well, she would see.

Eight

Candy was the first one down to the kitchen in the morning and started the bacon for breakfast. She put an apron over the simple jersey dress she had chosen to wear to the christening. It felt strange to be wearing nylons again. She had almost forgotten her other life as the debutante daughter of millionaire Evan Baylor.

Candy was soon joined by Charlie One Horse.

"Where's Garth?" he asked. "I figured the two of you would come in together for breakfast."

"I spent the night upstairs. I have no idea where Garth spent it. You're welcome to go find him. I'm cooking breakfast."

"Women," Charlie muttered. "Can't live with 'em, can't live without 'em."

They weren't alone for long. Jesse and Honey and Adam and Tate soon showed up with the babies. This time Honey's two gangly boys, Jack and Jonathan, were with them. Candy thought dinner the previous night had been chaos—breakfast was even less civilized.

Tate and Jesse starting tossing eggs back and forth. One of them missed, and Candy turned to find raw egg dripping down the front of the refrigerator. Shells lay cracked and broken on the tile floor, which was layered with a fine dusting of the flour Honey was using to make biscuits on the counter beside the stove. Both the babies were gurgling, and Madelyn was rocking their cradles, trying to keep the noise level down.

They took turns eating as the fried eggs were done. Charlie had already cracked two eggs into the pan for Faron when he realized Faron and Belinda hadn't come down yet.

"Tate, go call your brother," Charlie said.

Tate stepped to the kitchen doorway and yelled, "Faaarrrooon! Your eggs are done!"

"I could've done that," Charlie muttered.

Moments later Faron appeared. "I'm hungry as a bear. Where's my breakfast?"

"Still in the pan," Charlie replied.

"Where's Garth?" Faron asked Candy.

"Why ask me?" she retorted.

"I thought you two—"

"You thought wrong!" Candy said.

At that moment, Garth stepped into the kitchen from the interior hallway. Obviously he hadn't spent the night in the barn, either. He was dressed for church in a dark Western suit with a crisply ironed white shirt that set off his tanned skin and dark features. Lord, he was a good-looking man!

Candy pointedly turned her back on him and focused her attention on the stove.

She missed seeing the flash of pain in Garth's eyes, but Charlie One Horse did not. He shook his head in disgust and muttered, "Women."

Garth felt like a wounded animal, defensive, ready to lash out. He stared at his brothers and sister, daring them to say something, anything that would give him the excuse he was looking for to explode. Fortunately for all of them, Belinda chose that moment to make her entrance.

Every male eye in the room turned to stare at her. She had put her long blond hair up in an elegant twist, and she was wearing a sheath that outlined her figure, even though it concealed her from neck to knee.

"You look absolutely gorgeous," Tate said.

Faron slipped a protective arm around Belinda's waist and said, "And she's as nice as she is beautiful." He had obviously laid something other than a maternal claim to his stepmother, and was challenging his family to say anything about it.

This time it was Charlie One Horse who stepped in to diffuse the tension. He put a hand around Maddy's shoulder and said, "I 'spect I gotta vote that this here is the purtiest woman in the room."

Candy looked over her shoulder in time to see Maddy's blush. There could be no arguing that Charlie's compliment had made the grandmotherly woman glow.

Not to be outdone, Jesse announced, "Honey is the sweetest!"

Adam countered with, "Tate is the cutest."

That left Candy as the only woman in the room who hadn't been complimented. She stood by the stove, spatula in hand, staring at Garth and waiting.

Say it. Lay some claim to me. Name me yours, and I will be. Do it, Garth!

She willed him to speak, but he said nothing.

At last he turned to Tate. "We'd better get moving if we're going to be at the church on time. Finish up your breakfasts. I'll go get the car." He turned on his heel and stalked out the screen door, letting it slam behind him.

Candy's face paled. A moment later she left the kitchen with the excuse that she had to put on some more lipstick.

"But she hasn't eaten yet," Jesse protested.

Honey jabbed him in the ribs. "Hush."

When it came time to leave for church, there could be no doubt in anyone's mind that a rift had developed between Candy and Garth. She made a point of riding to church in a separate car. However, Faron maneuvered things so she was forced to sit in the pew beside Garth during the christening ceremony.

Candy had never been so aware of him. He was like a package of dynamite set to explode. All that was needed was a spark to set him off. Candy didn't intend to light that particular fire. She planned to ignore Garth for as long as it took to get back to the house and get her bags packed.

The incident this morning had finally made up her mind for her. Garth wasn't going to change. He could no more let go of the past than the black stallion that had refused to surrender his fear and his fury. She had learned everything she had come to learn. It was time to leave.

Only Garth apparently had other ideas.

Garth's family was celebrating the christening of Brett Patrick Philips with a picnic under the moss-laden live oak that shaded the back lawn. Candy stayed just long enough not to be rude, but excused herself from a game of softball that was forming and headed upstairs.

She was in her room packing when she heard someone knocking—pounding, really—on her door. Her heart began thumping with an equally powerful force.

"Who is it?"

"You know damned well who it is!" Garth shouted. "Open the door, Candy."

"I'm busy, Garth."

The door swung open so hard it crashed against the wall. She stood staring at him with wide, wary eyes.

He took one look at the suitcase on the bed and said, "What the hell do you think you're doing?"

What she was doing was perfectly obvious to both of them. "I'm packing."

"Why?"

Another stupid question. "Because I'm leaving."

"Starlight is in heavy labor. I need your help."

There were at least three men in the backyard who could have helped him, and she would have guessed that several of the Whitelaw women would have been equally capable of delivering a foal. Garth had the vet on call, as well. But she didn't point out to him the absurdity of his statement.

Candy supposed she owed Garth an explanation for why she could no longer remain at Hawk's Way. It wasn't going to be easy or pleasant making it, but it would allow her the mental peace she needed to get on with her life. A life without Garth Whitelaw.

She finished folding the jeans in her hands and laid them on top of the rest of the clothes in the suitcase. "All right, Garth. I'll come with you. We need to talk."

When he reached out to her, she avoided his hand. She could feel the tension in him as she crossed past him and out her bedroom door. "Have you called the vet?" she asked as they reached the bottom of the stairs.

"He's taking care of another emergency. He'll get here as soon as he can."

Candy felt a small chill of alarm. Maybe Garth's tension wasn't all directed at her. Maybe he was anticipating trouble. As she stepped through the screen door she said, "Maybe Faron or Jesse should be the one to help."

"There's nothing they know that I don't," Garth replied. It might have sounded like bragging if Candy hadn't known it was very likely the truth.

Candy stopped at the door to the barn. "What is it you need me for?" she demanded.

There was a long silence before he said, "You started this. I thought you should finish it."

His response was vague enough that he could have been referring to any number of things. "*You started this.*" Started *what?* The foaling of the mare? The taming of the stallion? Learning the art of breeding and training cutting horses? She suspected that where Garth was concerned, *this* referred to her relationship with him. Well, if he wanted to see a formal ending to the latter, she could and would provide it for him.

"All right, Garth," she said at last. "I'll see it to the end."

Her *it* was as vague as his *this*. Nevertheless, she was certain Garth understood her.

When Candy got a good look at the mare, her alarm increased. She turned to Garth and said, "She seems to be in a lot of pain, Garth. Is that normal?"

"Some pain is normal." He shoved a hand through his hair. "But not this much. There's something wrong." He whooshed out a breath of air. "I just hope the vet gets here in time to make a difference."

Candy realized suddenly why Garth had wanted her here. He was concerned about the mare. With his brothers or sister he would have had to maintain the stoic facade of uncaring. It was a mask he wore to hide his feelings—his very real and vulnerable feelings—from them. Last night had been a breakthrough of sorts. Today, for the first time— too late?—Garth was allowing her to see behind the mask.

A short half hour after Candy arrived at the barn, the mare went down. It was clear she was struggling to deliver the foal without much result.

"Shouldn't we call the vet again?" Candy asked, her fear apparent in her voice.

"He said he'd come when he can. Doc Stellan knows I wouldn't have called him if I didn't need him. He'll be here as soon as he can get here."

They were both sweating from the heat. Garth had his sleeves rolled up so he could check on the mare's progress occasionally. They left the mare momentarily alone in the stall so Garth could wash up at the sink in the barn.

"I should have called Doc Stellan the first time Starlight's labor stopped," Garth muttered to himself. "I shouldn't have waited."

"How could you have known?" Candy said, trying to ease his guilt.

"It's my job to know!" he snapped at her.

"You can't know everything!" she snapped right back.

"I sure as hell was mistaken about you," he retorted. "I thought you might be different. But you're just like every other woman—"

A screaming neigh cut him off.

"It's Starlight!" Candy cried.

The two of them set off running for the stall that contained the mare. For a moment they stood stunned.

Starlight lay on her side, clearly too exhausted to do what was necessary to complete the birth process. The tiny foal lay on the hay, still in its birth sac.

Candy had never seen Garth move so fast. He was on his knees beside the foal an instant later. He tore the sac away from the foal's mouth and nose with his hands and reached inside its mouth to clear the passage so the animal could breathe freely. But that wasn't enough.

"Breathe, damn you!" he demanded of the motionless form in his arms.

Meanwhile, Candy tended to the mare. Starlight was weak, but she was still alive. "Keep fighting, girl," she crooned to the mare. "You can make it. Keep fighting and everything will be all right."

Candy watched as Garth tried several ways to resuscitate the foal, even using his own breath to try and revive the tiny being. She could see now that the filly had a white star on its forehead that was an exact replica of the one Starlight bore.

At last Garth laid the foal down in the straw. His back was to Candy, so she couldn't see his face. But there was no mistaking the way his body heaved with silent grief. She stroked the mare the way she wanted to comfort him.

Until she realized the mare was also dead.

"Garth? *Garth?*"

Garth swiped at his eyes before he turned to face Candy. He saw the horror on her face and looked at the mare. Starlight had hemorrhaged, and he had been so busy with the foal that he hadn't noticed what was happening.

"She's dead, Garth. Starlight is dead."

"Hell. Dammit to hell!"

Candy wanted to hold Garth. She wanted to be held by him. But neither of them moved for what seemed a very long time.

"Candy, I—"

His dark eyes were full of so much pain. She crossed the distance between them on her knees. Then she was in his arms, and he was holding her tight, pressing kisses to her face and neck.

"Hold me," he said. "Hold me."

"I am. I will."

Candy didn't know how long they stayed like that. Her heart nearly broke when she felt his tears against her cheek. He *could* feel. He *did* care. Only he wasn't able to let his family see his vulnerability. He had needed to be strong, to hold his family together, to be a parent when his own parents were no longer there to do their jobs.

When at last he let her go, Candy searched out Garth's face, hoping the mask wouldn't be there. But the vulnerable man who had cried for the loss of a mare and a foal was gone. In his place was the Garth Whitelaw who wanted a woman for one purpose, and one purpose only.

In that moment she hated him. He had let her glimpse the man he could be, given her hope when she had been hopeless. And made it all the more difficult to say what she knew must be said.

"I'll be leaving in the morning."

"No one's stopping you."

That hurt. As he had known it would when he said it. Candy swallowed over the lump in her throat. "I want to thank you for everything you've taught me."

"There's more you have to learn," he said.

"It would take years to learn everything. I know enough to get started on my own. I thank you for that."

"Tell your father when you see him that he can send Comanche Moon here anytime it's convenient."

"Why would he send Comanche Moon here?"

"Your father and I had a little agreement."

Candy's lips flattened. "What sort of agreement?"

Garth shrugged negligently. "I agreed to teach you everything you wanted to know, and he agreed to sell me Comanche Moon at a fair price. The bargain is concluded the day you leave Hawk's Way."

"Were lessons in the bedroom part of the deal?" she asked in a scathing voice. "How could you? How could you blackmail my father that way?"

"He came to me," Garth countered. "And I'm paying a fair price for the horse."

"And that makes it all right?" she demanded. "I hate you! I don't think I could ever loathe anyone as much as I loathe you right now. I can't wait to get out of here!"

Candy surged to her feet and nearly fell again because her legs refused to hold her. Garth half rose to help her, and she shoved his hands away.

"Don't worry. You'll get what you bargained for. I'll make sure my father ships Comanche Moon here the instant I arrive home. Goodbye, Garth. And good riddance."

She left the barn at a walk, determined not to flee like the wounded animal she was. But her walk turned into a trot, and her trot into a run. She saw Garth's family as blurs of color as she sought out the safety of her room.

Garth stood unmoving for a long time. He didn't know why he had driven her away. He had come so close, so close to letting her see how much he cared for her. At the last instant he had turned away from the tenderness she had offered him. He was like that big black beast, unable to let go of the past. And it was destroying him, as it would one day destroy the beast.

Garth kept his distance from his family the rest of the day. He ordered Tom Handy to take care of removing the dead mare and foal. He was too afraid he might break down and cry if he saw them again. He called the vet and told him not to come.

Then Garth saddled up a horse and went riding across the vast acres of Hawk's Way, through canyons and gullies as he crisscrossed the rugged terrain. He rode without stopping until both he and the horse were exhausted.

It was nearly midnight when he arrived home. He breathed a sigh of relief when he saw the house was dark. There was a light on in the kitchen, but Charlie usually left a light burning in case someone got hungry during the night.

Garth was headed for the parlor and two long fingers of whiskey, but he ran head-on into Charlie One Horse when he stepped inside the kitchen door.

"Where you been?" the old man asked.

"Riding."

"Case you hadn't noticed, today was supposed to be a family celebration."

"I wasn't in much of a mood to celebrate," Garth said in a curt voice. "I lost Starlight and the foal both."

"Candy told me what happened."

Garth didn't want to ask, but he couldn't help himself. "Is she still here?"

"Where else would she be?"

Garth breathed a sigh of relief, although he knew he'd only had a reprieve, not a pardon.

"Women," Charlie muttered. "You gonna marry that girl?"

Garth's dark eyes were bleak. "She's decided to leave Hawk's Way."

"Mistake lettin' her get away."

"What am I supposed to do? Hog-tie her to keep her here?"

Charlie opened the refrigerator and began looking for something to snack on. "You admittin' you wanta keep her?"

"I want her," Garth said.

"You wanta marry her?" Charlie asked again.

"I want her," Garth repeated stubbornly.

Charlie shook his head again. "Gotta do better than that. Else you're gonna lose her sure. Can't get that filly without promisin' marriage. No sirree, Bob. With a girl like Candy, it's gotta be marriage or nothin'."

"You finished saying your piece, old man?"

"I'm finished."

"Then I'll be saying good night."

When Garth was gone, the old man shut the refrigerator door and stared at the ceiling. "Sure thought that filly had him lassoed good and tight. Ah, well, she ain't gone yet."

Meanwhile, Garth found the whiskey in the parlor and poured himself a glass without turning on a light. He crossed and sat in the leather chair before the fireplace and put his feet up on the rawhide stool that had held generations of Whitelaw boots. He stared into the glowing embers that were all that was left of what he was sure must have been a roaring fire earlier in the evening.

He sipped his whiskey trying to dull the pain. He thought about what Charlie had said. Would proposing marriage keep Candy Baylor from leaving tomorrow morning? He recalled the words she had shouted at him.

I hate you. I can't wait to get out of here!

Somehow he didn't think a marriage proposal would be very welcome right now.

Garth didn't know how long he had been sitting alone when Faron slumped into the leather chair beside him.

"What are you doing sitting here in the dark?" Faron asked.

"I could ask you the same thing," Garth responded.

"Women," Faron said in a tone reminiscent of the one Charlie One Horse had used.

Garth grunted an affirmation of the sentiment.

Neither of them said anything more, each caught up in his own thoughts. Occasionally, Garth drank from the glass of whiskey he held in his hand.

Without either of them knowing quite how it happened, Faron was spilling out his problems with Belinda Prescott. He had fallen in love with his stepmother but was unsure whether she loved him. They were both working hard to repair the ranch where Belinda lived so it could be sold, when all

Faron really wanted to do was marry Belinda and settle down at King's Castle and raise children.

Garth urged Faron to keep the ranch. And to pursue Belinda, if that was what he wanted.

"What are you doing hiding down here? I never thought you were a coward," Garth challenged.

Faron took enough umbrage to say, "I'm not the only Whitelaw sitting in the dark. What's the story between you and Candy Baylor?"

"None of your business," Garth said brusquely.

A slow smile grew on Faron's face. "Well, well, big brother. How the mighty have fallen."

"What's that supposed to mean?"

"You figure it out. I'm going upstairs where I hope there's a lady waiting for me. You can sit here alone in the dark all night if you want. But I suspect there might be a lady somewhere waiting for you, too."

"She'll have a long wait," Garth retorted.

Faron laughed. "Good night, Garth. Sleep well."

"Get out of here and leave me in peace."

"I'll leave, but I doubt you'll have much peace until you seek out a certain blond-haired, gray-eyed woman."

Hell and damnation! Garth wanted desperately to follow his youngest brother's advice. He wanted to go to Candy, to seek forgiveness, to beg her to stay. But that would mean admitting to her, and to himself, just how much he needed her. And that was still far too dangerous a proposition.

So he would have to let her go. When he thought of the life stretching out in front of him, it seemed bleak indeed.

Garth threw his whiskey glass against the stone hearth with all the pent-up anger and frustration he was feeling. The shattering glass sounded like an explosion in the silent house. He waited for his family to rouse, to come down and demand an explanation for his violent act.

But they slept on. Unaware of the turbulence in his mind and soul as the one women he had ever loved, would ever love, walked out of his life.

Tomorrow. Tomorrow before she left he would confront her one last time. He would tell her what he was feeling. He would lay his future happiness in her hands. He would give her his heart and wait to see if she broke it.

Nine

He was too late. When Garth knocked on Candy's door the next morning, she was already gone. Soon after that a long-distance call came for Faron and Belinda. A corporate buyer wanted to see King's Castle. They had to cut their visit short to return to Wyoming. Because the other two couples had driven to Hawk's Way from their southwest Texas ranches, they left right after lunch to try and miss the worst of the Labor Day traffic.

By late afternoon, Garth's family was gone from Hawk's Way, and he was alone. He avoided Charlie One Horse because he didn't want to hear the old man's "I told you so."

Since his brothers and sister had left the ranch and gone their own ways Garth had managed to keep the loneliness at bay. He had stayed busy, and having Charlie One Horse around gave things a sense of continuity. But after Labor Day that changed. Garth was aware there was something— someone—missing in his life. The days felt hollow, empty of all joy.

Within a week, Evan Baylor's prize stud arrived in a horse trailer, along with a note from Evan saying that once he received Garth's check for the agreed upon amount, their agreement would be fulfilled. Garth now had what he'd bargained for. But not what he wanted.

He wandered around Hawk's Way, trying to find a focus for his days, feeling the awful loneliness of the nights. For the next week, he couldn't seem to find the time to write that check to Evan Baylor. He had thought there was nothing that could make him change his mind about trusting a woman. He was discovering that in this, too, he had been mistaken.

Two weeks to the day after Candy had left him, Garth awoke with a purpose that drove him like a whip. "Hurry up with that breakfast, Charlie. I've got a lot of traveling to do today."

"You goin' someplace?"

"I'm taking Comanche Moon back to Evan Baylor."

Charlie gave Garth a speculative look. "You thinkin' 'bout makin' a trade?"

"I might be."

"Good idea," Charlie said. "You need that filly a lot more than you need that stud."

Garth grinned. "For once I have to agree with you."

The grin didn't stay on Garth's face for long. In fact, his look was downright grim by the time he arrived at Evan Baylor's doorstep. The drive to the B Bar Ranch outside of Dallas was long and grueling. The terrain was flat, the weather hot, and he had never seen a more welcome sight than Evan Baylor's Spanish hacienda.

The ranch house had thick, white-washed adobe walls that kept the heat out. He stepped through an arched doorway into a house that was dark and cool. The furniture consisted of heavy Mediterranean pieces accented by Navajo and Hopi Indian decorations. The living room was spacious and there were several arches inset along the walls adding to the Spanish flavor of the room.

Garth stood with his hat in his hand waiting to see Candy's father. He wasn't sure what his reception would be, but he was willing to insist that Evan Baylor talk to him.

Evan was cordial, if not friendly. "I'm surprised to see you, Garth. What's brought you over this way?"

"I've come to return Comanche Moon. I left him at the barn."

Evan arched a brow. "I always keep my bargains, Garth. You earned the horse. He's yours."

This time Garth heard the irritation in the older man's voice. "I didn't hold to my part of the bargain," Garth said.

"Oh?"

"I told your daughter about our agreement."

"Oh." Evan pinched the bridge of his nose. That explained Candy's cold behavior toward him for the past two weeks. She hadn't told him much about what had happened at Hawk's Way, except to say that she had learned a great deal. And that she never wanted to see Garth Whitelaw again for as long as she lived.

"I want to talk to her," Garth said.

"What makes you think she's here?"

There was a pause. Then, "Is she?"

Evan realized the futility of that sort of deceit. Garth would keep looking until he found her. "Candy doesn't want to see you."

"Too damn bad. I want to see her, and I won't take no for an answer."

"Now, look here, young man—"

"Either you ask her to come here, or I'm going to go hunting for her."

"Like hell!" Evan said. "You'll have to go through me first."

"If I have to, I will," Garth threatened.

"That won't be necessary."

Both men turned to face Candy, who was standing in one of the arched doorways. Garth had been hungry for the sight of her, and he ate her now with his eyes. He noticed changes in her appearance. There were smudges under her eyes that told him she hadn't been sleeping well, and her jeans hung on her, which told him she hadn't been eating right, either.

But her gray eyes flashed fire, and her chin jutted pugnaciously. She might have been bucked off, but she was raring to get right back on and apparently willing to use spurs, if that was what it took to stay there.

"I'll talk to him, Daddy."

"Do you want me to stay?" Evan asked.

Garth didn't bat an eyelash.

"No, Daddy. I'll be all right."

Evan looked from his daughter to the man who had come seeking her. "Call if you need me." Evan made it plain with a look he shot at Garth that although he was leaving them alone, he wasn't going far.

Candy followed her father's progress from the room, then turned to Garth. "Say what you came to say and get out."

Garth wasn't a man used to making explanations. Nor apologies. For Candy he was willing to do both. If only he could get the words out. But wanting to explain how he felt about her and being able to do so were two different things.

"I didn't figure you for a quitter." What he had intended as a compliment came out sounding more like a taunt.

"I'm not!" Candy retorted, stung into speaking.

Garth stared at her, trying to say with his eyes what he wasn't able to express in words.

I want you back at Hawk's Way. I need you in my life.

What he said was, "If you want to be the second-best wrangler in Texas, you've got a lot more to learn."

Candy bit down on an oath that sought voice. She had control of her temper. Barely. She wasn't going to allow Garth to provoke her into losing it. She was incensed by the mockery in Garth's voice and frustrated by the fact that he seemed determined to ignore the intimate relationship that had developed between them at Hawk's Way.

Candy had hoped and prayed every night since she left Hawk's Way that Garth would see the error of his ways. She had dreamed that he came after her and asked her to marry him. Well, he was here. But he wasn't following the script she had written for him. And she was just furious enough to take him up on his challenge.

"We'll just see who's a quitter!" She marched to the door through which her father had left and called, "Daddy! Come here, please!"

Evan came on the run. He looked worriedly from his daughter to the stony face of the man who had come to get her.

"I'm going back to Hawk's Way," she announced.

"Are you sure that's what you want to do? You aren't being forced or—"

"No one's forcing me into anything." She met Garth's glacial stare with fiery eyes. "I know exactly what I'm doing."

Candy hoped she was right. The risk of giving Garth a second chance was great, of course. But the rewards, if she could get past that cynical shell he used to protect himself, would be even greater. Just coming here, she realized, had been a huge step for Garth.

"I'll go pack a few things," she told Garth. "We can leave as soon as I'm done."

Once Candy was gone, Evan eyed Garth speculatively. "Would you like a drink?"

"I could use one," Garth admitted. "But I've got a lot of driving to do yet today."

"A cup of coffee?"

"That sounds good."

Evan led Garth into the decorated tile kitchen and poured him a cup of coffee from the pot on the stove. "Make yourself comfortable." He urged Garth to sit at the small wooden table set close to the wall and took the chair across from him.

"You broke my daughter's heart," he said.

"It wasn't my intention to hurt her."

"Yet you did," Evan said. "You'd better be damn sure of what you're doing, young man. Because you won't get another chance with my daughter."

Garth took that to mean Evan wouldn't allow it. He didn't argue with Candy's father. He took a sip of the coffee, which was hot enough to burn his tongue, and kept his thoughts to himself.

Evan was worried. Candy had been miserable in the two weeks since she had returned from Hawk's Way. His gentle probing had revealed little about what had happened to bring her home. She had mentioned Garth but had refused to discuss the man. Garth's arrival explained a lot of things Evan had been wondering about.

Obviously his daughter and Garth Whitelaw had been having a love affair. It was difficult as a father to allow Candy to leave again with the wrangler. But she was a grown woman, and she knew what she wanted. Evan had always known he was going to lose his daughter someday. He would never know what Candy saw in a man as hard as Garth Whitelaw. But then, Evan hadn't known why his wife, Roberta, had chosen him, either. Nonetheless, they had enjoyed a loving and happy relationship for as long as Roberta had lived.

Evan interpreted Garth's sudden appearance at the B Bar as a good sign. The fact that Garth had returned the stallion was an even better sign. The young man's insistence on seeing Candy and his refusal to be deterred from his purpose was the best sign of all. Evan needed those signs to justify letting his daughter go with this man who had hurt her so terribly. He hoped Candy knew what she was doing. Because Evan was sure Garth Whitelaw had the power to break his daughter's heart.

"I'm ready," Candy said, joining them in the kitchen.

Garth rose and took the suitcase from her. "I left the truck at the barn." At Candy's questioning look he added, "I brought Comanche Moon back."

"He didn't keep his part of the bargain," Evan explained. "He told you I arranged for him to teach you in exchange for the horse."

"Was that all you arranged?" Candy asked.

Evan looked hurt that she would even ask. "Absolutely."

"We'd better leave if we're going to get back to Hawk's Way tonight," Garth said.

There wasn't much to see once it got dark, and neither of them wanted to listen to the radio. Candy sat with her arm resting on the open window, staring out at the shadowy landscape.

"I've been doing a lot of thinking since you left Hawk's Way," Garth said at last.

"Oh?" Candy's heart began to beat a little faster.

"I . . . I've blamed every woman I ever met for what my mother did to my father."

Candy remained silent.

Garth swallowed over the knot in his throat and kept talking. "I always figured that if I never let myself love a woman, she could never hurt me."

"So you never loved anyone," Candy said in a soft voice. *Not even me?* she wanted to ask. That was entirely too dangerous a question. The fact that Garth had come after her was significant. It didn't mean he had let go of the past. Only that he wanted to try.

Neither of them said anything more until they could see the lights of Hawk's Way in the distance. Candy turned to Garth and said, "What is it you want from me, Garth?"

I want you to love me. But he couldn't yet say that to her aloud. "I don't know," he said gruffly. "I want you. I always have." *I always will.*

Candy sighed. Trust a man to focus on the physical. "That isn't enough, Garth."

"I know," he admitted with a sigh easily as large as her own.

Candy took a deep breath and asked, "Do you really think you can change?"

Garth met her eyes with a bleak look. "I don't know."

It might not have been a very satisfying answer, but it was an honest one. Candy realized that only the test of time would tell whether Garth could put the past behind him.

When they arrived at Hawk's Way, Charlie One Horse was nowhere to be seen. Garth carried Candy's suitcase up to her room—the one next to his. She looked at him askance, but he did no more than set down the suitcase and back away to the door.

"You know where everything is," he said. Then he closed the door between them.

Candy frowned. She knew Garth had been aroused. She had seen the glitter in his dark eyes, the tautness of his body when he passed by her, not to mention the ridge in his jeans. Yet he hadn't tried to seduce her. She was confused by his restraint. But not discouraged.

In fact, Garth's unusual behavior continued over the next several days and weeks. His eyes never left her, and when she caught his glance the heat was enough to warm her deep inside. But they continued tiptoeing around each other, afraid to wreck the fragile balance in their relationship.

Candy went back to work with the black stallion. She got up before dawn each day to make time for an extra session with the animal. She was close to earning his trust. She just knew it!

At last the day came when she held out her hand, and the stallion walked up to take the cube of sugar from her. Of course he instantly danced away again. But if he had done it once, Candy knew that sooner or later he would do it again. It was only the first step, but it was a big one.

"I didn't think that would ever happen."

Candy whirled to find Garth directly behind her. She smiled up at him. "He's a lot like you."

"How's that?"

"Afraid to trust."

Garth stiffened. Candy had just stepped over the invisible line they had drawn regarding discussion of their relationship. "I suppose next you'll be holding out a cube of sugar to me," he said in an acid voice.

"I would if I thought it would sweeten you up any," she retorted. When she tried to leave, Garth caught her wrist and snapped her back around to face him.

"Where are you going?" he demanded, terrified that she might be leaving him again.

"I have work to do."

"Nothing that can't wait." Garth had stayed away from Candy as long as he could. Simply touching her had brought back memories of how she felt in his arms. "Come with me." He paused and added, "Please."

"When you put it that way," she said, "I find myself inclined to join you."

Garth picked her up in his arms and headed for the house.

"Garth!" she said with a breathless laugh. "Everyone will see us."

"Let them look. I don't care."

He took the stairs two at a time, and by the time he reached his room, Candy was as aroused as he was. When Garth let her feet go, she laced her hands around his neck and urged his head down for her kiss.

The first touch of Garth's lips sent a shiver through Candy.

"Garth."

It was all she said, but it was enough to send the blood pumping through Garth's body. He wasn't feeling patient, but he forced himself to slow down. His mouth trailed over her temple, down her cheek to her ear. Her head fell back and he kissed her throat. He sucked hard enough to put a love bruise on her, branding her as his. It was a savage, primitive thing to do, but he wasn't feeling very civilized at the moment.

Candy wasn't aware of the pain, only the pleasure of Garth's mouth on her flesh. Sensation streaked through her, until she was quivering with desire.

They shed their clothes like winter coats in springtime, and then they were standing naked before each other.

"You are so beautiful," Garth said as he reached out reverently to cup her breasts. He lowered his head to suckle her, and Candy's whole body arched toward him.

Her hands landed low on his hips and slid around to his buttocks. Her fingernails left crescents as she held on for dear life.

Garth picked her up and laid her on the bed, mantling her body with his. Moments later he was inside her. She was wet and tight and welcoming.

"You have no idea how wonderful this feels," he said with a satisfied groan.

"Oh, I think I do," Candy said. She moaned deep in her throat.

Garth put his hands on either side of Candy's face and forced her to look at him. His voice was fierce, his dark eyes savage. "Don't ever leave me again, Candy. I need you."

It wasn't a declaration of love, but Candy suspected it was as close to one as Garth Whitelaw had ever come. She put her hands on either side of his face. "I love you, Garth."

She was afraid he would turn away from the words, as he had in the past. This time his face bore a look of exultation.

Garth didn't say anything more. Neither did she. But there was something different about this loving. Something deeper. More powerful. More moving than anything that had passed between them before.

Afterward, they lay close in each other's arms, until their panting eased and they could speak again.

"Will you spend the night here with me?" Garth asked.

Candy remembered what Garth had said when she had first asked him why he had never married. *Why buy the cow when the milk's free?* But she couldn't bring herself to leave him. If he didn't love her enough to marry her, she would know soon enough. And if that turned out to be the case...

She might not have a lifetime with Garth; she might have only the next few days or weeks. She planned to make a lifetime of memories for the day when she might be forced to leave him.

Candy snuggled closer to Garth and laid her arm across his chest. She angled her nose under his chin until she was comfortable and said, "I'll stay."

Garth pulled her snug against him. This felt right. It felt good. Surely it was safe to love her. Surely he would find a way to convince her that she belonged with him without having to say the words. Because it simply wasn't possible for him to speak them. It ought to be enough to prove to her how he felt.

Garth fell asleep trying to convince himself that Candy didn't—wouldn't—need to hear the words to know he loved her.

Ten

———

Candy succeeded beyond her wildest expectations with the black stallion. In a matter of weeks, he was not only coming to her for sugar, but she had put a halter on him and was leading him around.

"I think I'll call Señor Santos and tell him I've decided to collect on the fee he offered me, after all," Garth said when he caught Candy standing inside the corral stroking the stallion's neck.

"What fee?"

"He said if I could get Midnight to stand at stud I could breed him to the mare of my choice."

Candy stammered, "B-but we don't know how he'd act with a mare. He might savage her."

Garth grinned. "I don't think so. Midnight's problem was with humans. Nobody could handle him to get him close to a ready mare. I feel certain he'd know what to do if the situation arose."

"But—"

Garth's voice hardened. "I say he's ready. I'm going to have him cover Starlight's firstborn tomorrow afternoon."

Candy paled. Since the death of Starlight and her second foal, Candy had sought out Starlight's firstborn, a five-year-old mare out of Starlight by Hawk's Sanctuary. The mare's name was Hawk's Star and she was beautiful, a rich glossy black, with a star on her forehead. Candy had befriended the horse, and although she would have been more than happy for Midnight to prove himself, she didn't want it to be with Hawk's Star.

The thought of the savage stallion covering the mare left her feeling physically ill. "I'm afraid," she said.

"Of what?" Garth asked.

"That he'll hurt her."

"I admit the mating of two horses sounds wild and brutal, but it isn't usually. I'll keep an eye on Midnight to make sure he doesn't get vicious with Hawk's Star."

Candy swallowed hard and said, "If you're going to be there, then I want to be there, too."

Garth eyed her sharply. "Are you sure?"

"Midnight knows me best. He'll respond best to me if it's necessary to separate the two horses."

Garth snorted. "Once he's with her, his mind won't be on leaving."

"Nevertheless," Candy said, "I want to be there."

For someone who wanted to possess her own stable and breed her own stock, Candy had been strangely reluctant to observe the mating of stallion and mare. She had studied Garth's stud books to see which stallions he put with which mares, and looked to see the results in their offspring. She understood what assets Garth was looking for in an animal, and how he chose one horse to be bred to another.

But it seemed profane somehow to stand by and watch while a stallion covered a mare, even though she knew it was done for the protection of both animals. The mare might lash out with her hooves at the stallion, or he might savage her in return. In the wild, one animal could run away from the other. In a corral, there was no escape. The humans who had put them there together had to rescue the one that needed help.

It didn't help her peace of mind when Candy discovered the next afternoon that Hawk's Star had never been bred before.

"She'll be scared. She'll fight him!"

"No she won't," Garth reassured her. "She's ready. I've had them in side-by-side corrals all morning. She's been flirting with that stud like a two-dollar—" Garth cut off the vulgar reference he had been going to make and finished, "She's been flirting with him all morning."

"She's so small," Candy protested.

"She'll be fine."

"He looks so wild."

"He'll settle down."

"It's her first time."

"There has to be a first time for everyone."

The sexual tension in the animals had been transmitted to the humans. Candy's body felt stretched and full, and she was aware of every move Garth made. She wanted him, had unconsciously sent out sensual lures to him all day. Like the mare, she teased Garth and then moved away, making it necessary for him to follow her.

Garth's mouth was dry as a bone. His body was strung taut as barbed wire. He wasn't sure if Candy was aware of how she was teasing him, taunting him, but he damned sure wasn't going to wait much longer to do something about it.

If the truth were known, Garth was as anxious about putting the two animals together as Candy was. The difference was, he had previously observed the wildness, the naked ferocity of the act that was coming. She had not.

Garth opened the gate, and Candy led Midnight inside the small breeding corral. She left the halter on Midnight so he would be easier to catch, but disconnected the lead. She stepped out, and Garth closed the gate behind her. Tom Handy was there to help, if help was needed.

But Hawk's Star wasn't in the least shy. And Midnight knew exactly what he wanted. The stallion quickly covered the mare. Even with both horses willing, Candy was unprepared for the violence of the coupling. She couldn't bear to stay and watch. She headed for the house at a brisk walk. As soon as she was out of Garth's sight, she broke into a run.

Garth was torn between his duty to stay and his desire to go.

"I'll keep an eye on the horses," Tom offered.

Garth nodded abruptly and headed in the direction Candy had gone. Charlie's truck was missing, so he knew there was no one else in the house besides Candy. Garth ran up the stairs and stopped to catch his breath in front of Candy's bedroom door.

"Candy? I'm coming in." Garth didn't wait for an invitation because he wasn't sure he would get one. Candy was curled up on her bed, her face hidden in her pillow. He sat down beside her and touched her shoulder. "Candy?"

The instant he touched her she turned and launched herself into his arms. "Oh, Garth!"

Garth had never had much to do with crying women and now he knew why. A man felt downright helpless in the face of a woman's tears. All he could do was hold her tight and tell her everything would be all right. Garth felt her anguish, and if there had been a way to do it, he would have taken her pain on himself. He had to be content with murmuring words of comfort.

"Even though it looks wild and rough, the coupling isn't hurtful to the mare," he said.

Garth pushed the hair back from Candy's face and kissed her brow. Then he kissed away the tears at the corners of her eyes and on her cheeks, until his lips found their way to her mouth.

It was the gentlest, the softest kiss Candy had ever felt, and it touched her to her core. A steady warmth built inside her. She shivered when she heard the stallion's neighing scream and the mare's sharp whinny in reply.

Candy looked into Garth's dark eyes and saw a fierceness there every bit as savage as the stallion. And like the mare, she had no intention of denying him. Candy returned Garth's kisses with an urgency she didn't understand. She only knew it was necessary to couple with Garth now, to love him as she had never loved him before. Because time, her precious time with him, was finally running out.

"Love me, Garth. Please, love me." It was a plea from the heart, an urgent wish not just for the physical act, but for an emotional commitment.

Garth didn't answer her in words. She hadn't expected him to. He stripped her and himself and laid her out naked for his admiration.

"You are so perfect," Garth said in a husky voice. "Your breasts high and firm. Your belly flat. Your legs strong and slender."

He worshipped her with words. His hands adored her. His mouth cherished her. His loving was as tender as it had ever been.

But the passions running high between them put tremendous pressure on Garth's restraint. Until at last he gave rein to the demands of his nature. Man's possession of his mate was every bit as violent as that of any other animal.

Candy arched up to receive Garth as he covered her with his body. She gasped as his thrust impaled her. Her hands clutched at his shoulders as he began to move inside her. Candy was insensate with desire as she undulated beneath him.

Her fingers clawed at him.

His hands grasped at her.

Her legs circled him and held on.

His mouth claimed hers and clung.

At the moment of ultimate pleasure, Candy's wild cry of fulfillment urged Garth to his own release. His shout of exultation was no less feral than hers.

The tumultuous coupling expressed all the unspoken love each felt for the other. But in the aftermath, only she was able to say the words that expressed what they had shared.

"I love you, Garth."

There was a long silence, one that begged for words of response. Candy waited. But Garth remained silent.

Candy lay in his arms and felt only despair. Her dream that Garth would one day love her seemed doomed to remain unfulfilled. Oh, he could desire her. And he could demonstrate that desire. But because of his past, he was unable to trust—ultimately to love—any woman. She had to face the fact that he never would and go on with her life.

Candy slipped out of Garth's embrace and left the bed, looking for the clothes he had scattered when he had torn them from her.

Garth's eyes were closed, his body completely relaxed. He was enjoying the languor of a sexually satisfied male. He was aware Candy had left the bed, but he expected her to return at any moment. His arms felt empty without her. He knew she had wanted him to speak his love aloud. But it was still a very new emotion, and he felt too vulnerable to say the words.

But he knew now that he loved her. He felt almost giddy with the knowledge. Someday he might even be able to tell her so. Garth took a breath and let it out.

When Garth felt the weight on Candy's side of the bed, he thought she was returning. Then he heard two clicks. He shot bolt upright and stared at what he found.

Candy was completely dressed. She was packing her suitcase to leave.

He grabbed for his jeans and yanked them on, leaving them half-unbuttoned as he stalked around the bed to confront her. "What the hell do you think you're doing?"

"I think it's pretty obvious what I'm doing. I'm packing."

"Why?"

"I'm leaving."

"Why?"

Candy closed her eyes and took a deep breath. She let it out, opened her eyes and said, "I thought I could wait forever for you to love me. I can't. It hurts too much."

"I care for you," Garth managed to say.

"Oh, Garth." Candy knew it was more than he had ever said to any woman. But it wasn't enough upon which to build a lifetime together. "That's not enough," she said at last.

"What do you want from me?" he demanded. "I've done everything I can to show you how I feel," he said in a savage voice.

"I want the words. I want you to say it out loud. I wouldn't even mind if you shouted it to the heavens," she said with a sad, wry smile.

But Garth said nothing.

Candy returned to packing.

Garth wanted to rip the clothes from her hands. Wanted to throw the suitcase across the room. Wanted to fold her in his arms and never let her go.

He watched her close the suitcase and snap it shut on the bed. When she walked out that door, he would lose her forever.

Garth faced a moment of truth. He had to let go of the past—or let go of Candy. When it came right down to it, the choice was amazingly easy.

"I love you, Candy."

The words had a harsh, grating sound, but they were the sweetest Candy had ever heard. She stared at Garth, her heart in her throat. She was afraid to believe what she had heard. "Say it again."

"I love you."

"I wasn't hearing things?"

"No, you weren't. I love you, Candy."

"Oh, Garth!" She launched herself into his arms from halfway across the room. He caught her and swung her around with abandon. His mouth found hers and his tongue thrust inside, laying claim to her.

"You're mine, now," he rasped. "Now and forever."

"And you're mine," she said just as fiercely. "Now and forever."

"We'll have children, lots of them," he promised.

"Oh, I hope so," she said. "In fact, I think we already have one on the way."

Garth stared at her, stunned even though he had always known it was a possibility. "What?"

Candy laughed. "I said we already have one on the way."

Garth sobered, only now realizing just how much had been at stake. And how close he had come to losing it all. He would never take that chance again. He would say the words often, until Candy would never again doubt his love.

"I love you, Candy."

"And I love you, Garth. Everything will be all right. You'll see."

He took her to bed again. This time the loving was tender. At the moment of climax he said the words that sealed their fates together.

"I will always love you," the wrangler promised her.

"As I will love you, always and forever," the rich girl promised in return.

Epilogue

___

"Eight—uh—nine months later you was born, Zach. Three months after that, Hawk's Star foaled a fine colt with a star on his forehead."

"And Mom named him Midnight Star," Falcon piped up.

"Yessiree, that's the one." Charlie One Horse looked down at the little girl asleep in his arms. Zach lay sprawled on the floor in front of the fireplace. Falcon sat cross-legged at Charlie's feet. "And that's the story of how your mom and dad met and fell in love."

Zach rolled over to face his father and asked, "Is that how it really happened, Dad?"

Garth kissed Candy softly on the mouth and said, "Trust your uncle Charlie, boy. It happened just the way he said. I took one look at your Mom, and I knew she was the woman for me. Now it's time for all of you to get to bed."

"Do we hafta?" Falcon asked.

"You can barely keep your eyes open," Candy chided. "Come on now."

She herded the two boys ahead of her while Garth retrieved his daughter from Charlie's lap.

"She's sleepin' like an angel," Charlie said as he gave up his burden. The old man marveled at how tenderly Garth held the girl. He wanted to be a fly on the wall when the first beaus came calling on Callen Whitelaw.

Garth caught up with Candy and slipped his arm around her waist. Charlie heard them laughing together as they followed their sons up the stairs.

"Yep," Charlie muttered to himself as he watched them disappear, "that sure is the way it happened, all right. And the wrangler and the rich girl lived happily ever after."

* * * * *